CHEERLEADERS

#34

COMING BACK

LISA NORBY

SCHOLASTIC INC.
New York Toronto London Auckland Sydney

ISBN 0-590-40999-9

12 11 10 9 8 7 6 5 4 3 2 1   7 8 9/8 0 1 2/9

Printed in the U.S.A   01

First Scholastic printing, October 1987

CHEERLEADERS

COMING BACK

CHEERLEADERS

CHAPTER

"Tell us, Olivia Evans, what is your greatest fear?"

Olivia glared at the tiny microphone that was being held in front of her lips, then up at the laughing eyes of David Duffy.

"What does that have to do with an interview about college finances?" she protested.

"Nothing," admitted Duffy with a shrug. "I just wondered. But if you don't like that question, we'll go on to another one. How about telling me your secret ambition, or your favorite fantasy?"

"Duffy!"

"Okay, I'll try to be more specific. Why don't you tell me what you look for in a guy. Describe your ideal of masculine appeal. Please feel free to be influenced by the fine specimen you see before you." Duffy had her backed into a corner by the water fountain and was peering down at her, his face a mask of mock sincerity.

1

Olivia suppressed a giggle. "Nice try, Duffy, but not now," she said. "I was due at practice five minutes ago. I don't have time to kid around."

Duffy looked wounded. "Who's kidding? It isn't every young woman who rates a personal in-depth interview with David Duffy, future network sports commentator extraordinaire. I'm completely serious. I want to know all about you."

"Duffy, you already do know all about me. We've been dating for months."

"I don't think I do," Duffy said, suddenly serious. "There are lots of times when I think I do. Then I look at you, and I catch this faraway expression on your face, and I realize that Olivia Evans is still pretty much of a mystery to me."

"Seriously?"

"Absolutely seriously." Duffy held up two fingers. "Scout's honor."

Olivia knew that the way to end the conversation and get away to cheerleading practice would be to tell Duffy what he wanted to hear — that *he* was her ideal man. But somehow, she couldn't bring herself to say it.

Maybe the problem was that it was close to being true. Duffy was certainly the most romantic guy she had never known. She liked his lean, angular face; his great clothes; and the way he always smelled faintly of some sort of tweedy men's cologne. Compared to the boys in her class, Duffy often seemed very sophisticated and romantic, and he certainly knew how to make a girl feel special.

Still, it bothered her that she often had no

idea whether Duffy was being serious. She often wondered if he knew, either. Words came so easily to Duffy that she suspected that they sometimes ran ahead of his feelings.

Olivia, on the other hand, had never been comfortable putting her deeper feelings into words. It was flattering that Duffy thought she was mysterious. But she couldn't help wondering how long it would take him to discover that she was just plain shy.

"Can't we finish talking about this after practice?" she said finally. "Besides, you probably should interview some other students. I'm sure your editor knows that we date, and he must get tired of seeing my name in every story you write about Tarenton High."

"You're still the captain of the Varsity Cheerleading Squad," Duffy pointed out. "That makes you a class leader. He doesn't expect me to ignore you."

"Okay. But if you want to interview one of the cheerleaders about scholarships, the person you ought to talk to is Hope Chang. I know she's only a junior, but she's the one who has her heart set on going to an exclusive private college. And even with her grades and all her activities, she's still worried she won't be able to get a scholarship."

"That's not a bad idea," Duffy admitted. "I think I will talk to her. But what about us? I still want to know more about the private thoughts of Olivia Evans."

Olivia glanced anxiously at her watch. "If I answer one question now, will you let me go?"

3

"It's a deal."

"Fine. My greatest fear is that I'm going to mess up in my job as cheerleading captain. I'm late for practice already, and if you don't let me go right now, it's going to be more than just a fear."

"Whatever you say." Duffy stepped aside, and Olivia realized from the surprised look on his face that it hadn't dawned on him before that she was serious about wanting to get away. "I didn't mean to keep you from practice, honest," he told her. "But don't you think you're being just a little bit paranoid? I mean, what difference does it make if you're a few minutes late? No one will notice."

Normally, Duffy would have been right. But on that particular afternoon Olivia's late arrival was very much noticed. Several members of the squad had heavy tests coming up the next day. Sean Dubrow, in particular, had a study date with his girl friend Kate Harmon, and he was counting on her to explain six weeks of trigonometry to him in one evening.

Even the cheerleaders' coach, Ardith Engborg, was unusually eager to get the afternoon's practice over with early. Coach Engborg had been feeling slow and grouchy all day, and in the short break between her last class and the beginning of practice she retreated to her office and tried to revive herself by brewing a cup of tea.

Out on the floor, the rest of the squad were already in their practice clothes and ready to start their warm-ups. Hope Chang, the first to arrive, as usual, had already done some stretching exercises on her own and was starting to look anxious. "I wonder where Olivia is," she said. "I have a lot of chemistry to study tonight."

Brown-haired, green-eyed Jessica Bennett stared at Hope in amazement. She and Hope happened to be in the same chemistry lab section, and she knew that Hope was far and away the best student in class. "What can you possibly have left to study?" she wailed. "Can't you take pity on the rest of us? You'll just make us look even dumber than we are!"

"Hope's right," said Sean, flashing a dazzling smile in her direction. "I took time out of my busy schedule to be here, so why can't Olivia be here on time? If you ask me, she's letting David Duffy become too much of a distraction. I saw him around school earlier this afternoon, and I'm sure that's why Olivia isn't here."

"You're one to talk, Dubrow," said Peter Rayman, the other male member of the squad. "When it comes to being distracted by the opposite sex, you hold the record."

Tara Armstrong had been off to one side doing a few minutes of aerobics to get up her energy level. "Instead of squabbling," she suggested, "why don't we use this time to discuss the new routine we're supposed to be learning today?" She shook her lush, auburn hair into place and grabbed a photocopied description of the routine that Olivia had passed out at their last practice. "Isn't there someone besides me who thinks this is a little bit too complicated? Especially this part where we have the cartwheels, then a back walk-over. . . ."

"That doesn't sound so difficult to me!" Jessica cut in.

With the possible exception of Olivia, Jessica was the best gymnast on the squad. She hadn't meant the remark to be a put-down of Tara, but after the words were out she realized that they had sounded that way.

"It isn't that I can't do them," Tara said, looking annoyed. "I was just wondering whether they serve any purpose. These aren't the Olympic try-outs. We're supposed to be team spirit leaders. What's the point of having so many fancy moves that they interfere with the rhythm of the cheer? I just don't see why we need to show off!"

"Look who's talking about showing off!" groused Jessica.

"Wait a second," said Peter. "I think Tara has a point. We could do a lot more with choreography. A lot of our routines are just one stunt after another."

From inside her office, Coach Engborg could see but not hear the discussion. She had been tempted to call off practice and leave school early, but had stayed around because she didn't want to short-change the squad. Now she was rapidly becoming disgusted. It was bad enough that Olivia was late, but what really irked her was that none of the other cheerleaders took the initiative to get things started.

Pushing aside her mug of tea, Coach Engborg got up from her desk and strode out onto the gym

6

floor. "Sometimes you guys are as bad as the grade school softball teams I used to coach," she told them. "Those little kids would play half an inning and then spend the rest of the afternoon arguing about the umpire's calls."

"We were discussing the new routine," Peter explained.

"There's no point in talking about it until you've at least tried it," Ardith Engborg pointed out.

"But Olivia isn't here yet!"

"All right, then I'll run through Olivia's part."

"You!" Sean gasped.

The coach turned and stared at him, her hands on her hips. "Do you think I can't, young man? I'm not exactly ready for the rocking chair yet."

"I didn't mean that, Coach," Sean said. "But the routine starts with a couple of lifts. . . ."

"So?"

Sean Dubrow was not easily embarrassed, but for some reason the thought of having to partner Coach Engborg made him writhe with embarrassment. What if she couldn't do the lifts? What if he dropped her?

Reluctantly, he put his hands around the coach's waist and lifted her off the ground. After the first few seconds, however, his fears evaporated. Although the coach looked anything but elegant in her baggy warm-up pants and turtleneck sweater, she had a lot more spring in her leaps than he would have guessed.

As the coach did a perfect dismount from Sean's shoulders, there were even a few scattered cheers.

"Okay, what comes next?" she called out to Tara.

Tara checked the photocopied sheet of instructions. "Two cartwheels," she called out.

The first cartwheel the coach did was perfect. On the second, she wobbled a bit but managed to regain her balance. Then, quite suddenly, she grimaced in pain and collapsed onto the mat.

The squad was so stunned that for a few seconds everyone just stood there as if they were paralyzed. No one was quite sure what had happened, much less what to do about it.

Tara was the first to find her voice. "Stay calm, everyone," she shrieked. "Someone call an ambulance. Then we have to do CPR. I saw it done on TV once. I think it was on a rerun of *Benson*."

"That's the Heimlich Maneuver," snapped Peter.

Coach Engborg opened her eyes. "It's a good thing I *don't* need CPR."

Everyone was so relieved that they all started shouting at once: "Coach!" "Are you all right?" "What happened?"

"It's just my knee. It's the old problem; I thought the last operation would take care of it, but I think this time I've really done a job on it."

"What should we do?" asked Hope. "Do you think we should call a doctor or an ambulance?"

"That won't be necessary," said Coach Engborg. "But I would appreciate it if someone could drive me to the hospital. The last time this happened, my orthopedist warned me that if it happened again, I'd probably need surgery —

again — and I'm sure she'll want me to have X rays."

She tried to get to her feet, but Sean stopped her. "I'll drive you. But wait a second," he said. "I think there's a wheelchair in the nurse's station. Let me see if I can get someone to let me in there."

A few minutes later, Sean was flying down the hall, pushing the empty wheelchair ahead of him, when he ran into Olivia. "What's wrong?" she gasped. "Did someone get hurt?"

"It's the coach," Sean told her. "She was demonstrating your routine and she did something to that trick knee of hers. It looks pretty serious."

Olivia ran back into the gym and stood there helplessly as Peter and Jessica helped Coach Engborg into the wheelchair. Hope and Tara collected the coach's street clothes and purse from her office.

"Is there anything I can do?" Olivia asked helplessly.

"Not really," said Ardith Engborg. "Since everyone seems to have other things to do this evening, anyway, why don't you all just forget about practice for today? I'll get in touch with you tomorrow."

As Sean wheeled the coach out of the gym, Olivia noticed the clock on the wall. She was only ten minutes late. How could all this have happened so quickly?

"It wasn't my fault. Honest!" she said to no one in particular.

Jessica shook her head. "Did anyone say it was your fault?"

No one had. But Olivia couldn't help suspecting that was exactly what everyone else was thinking. If only she had been on time, Coach Engborg would never have tried to do that routine and gotten hurt.

Dejectedly, she left the gym and caught up with Duffy, who was still interviewing seniors for his *Tarenton Lighter* article. "Remember what I said about my worst fear?" she asked him. "I think it just came true."

CHAPTER

After they had finished changing into their street clothes, Tara and Hope walked out to the parking lot together. "You can't put it off any longer," Tara was saying.

"Yes, I can," insisted Hope. "I have a lot of studying to do."

"You have plenty of time. Besides, you would have been in practice for another hour if it hadn't been called off."

"I suppose you're right." Hope sighed and took the car keys that Tara was dangling in front of her nose.

"You ought to be grateful," Tara reminded her. "How many friends would let you drive their car?"

None of them, at this point, Hope reminded herself. She had already renewed her learner's permit once, and so far she had gone through four driving instructors. First, her father had taught her the basics, but after the first time he tried to show her how to parallel park, Hope ended up in tears. After that episode, Hope complained that her father's criticisms made her nervous, and Mr. Chang had turned the driving lessons over to his wife.

But with Hope's mother, there had been the opposite problem. Watching her daughter drive made Mrs. Chang so jumpy that she thought she was actually a menace. As soon as she saw a light turn red up the block, Mrs. Chang would hiss, "Watch out!" and Hope, naturally, would step on the brakes. Once, this happened right on the main street of Tarenton when a local police car was traveling right behind them. Fortunately, the police officer had managed to stop in time, and he was very understanding when he saw that Hope was a new driver.

After her mother decided not to give her any more lessons, Hope signed up with the driving school at Grove Lake. But two weeks ago, her instructor there had refused to give her any more lessons. "There's nothing wrong with your driving," he told her. "You're ready to take the test, and it wouldn't be right to take your money for more lessons."

Still, Hope didn't *feel* ready. The thought of the driving test terrified her, and Tara had generously offered to give her a few more practice sessions in the Chevy.

Tara had thought that coaching Hope to pass her test would be kind of fun, but after just a few attempts she was already beginning to change her mind. "I think the U-Drive Auto School was right," she told Hope, as they practiced parallel parking in the empty school lot. "You are ready to take that test. You just have some kind of fixation about it."

"Maybe," admitted Hope. "It's just that having a driver's license is so much responsibility."

Tara bit her lip to keep from laughing out loud. Hope was wearing a tweed chesterfield coat, the kind with black velvet trim on the collar. And under that, she had on a pink turtleneck sweater; a gray A-line skirt; nylons; and neat, classically styled pumps. She was the picture of responsibility — so much so that Tara, with her jeans and boots and big gold hoop earrings, felt like a wild child by comparison.

"Hope, have you ever looked at some of the people who are driving cars?" Tara asked her as they pulled out onto the main road. "You are at least as responsible as most of them. Even more so."

Hope didn't find this the least bit comforting. "That just makes me more nervous," she confessed. "Besides worrying about what I'm doing, I have to worry about them, too."

Tara groaned. "Forget it. Just drive."

"Where to?"

"Anywhere. Just drive around."

"I can't drive if I don't know where I'm going!"

Tara wanted to scream. "Okay," she said, "head for that twenty-four-hour convenience store on Parker Road. We can pick up a soda there."

13

They were about two miles from their destination when Hope exclaimed, "Hey, did you see that?"

"What? I didn't see anything!"

While Tara looked around in confusion, Hope slowed the car, pulled over onto the shoulder of the road, and began backing up. "What are you doing?" Tara wailed. "You can't drive on the shoulder of the road! You'll get us stuck in the mud."

But for the first time since she took the wheel, Hope was completely calm. She backed up expertly and steered into a pull-off that overlooked Grove Lake. Then she turned off the engine and got out of the car. "Wait here," she ordered Tara.

A few minutes later she returned, clutching a very cute but very dirty puppy. "Look at this little fellow," she cooed. "He's too little to be out here on his own all night. How did he get way out here? There isn't a house anywhere around."

"You're not planning to bring that animal into the car?" Tara asked, alarmed. "He'll ruin the upholstery. Your coat is already a mess. Besides, who knows what kind of diseases he's got?"

"Don't be silly," Hope told her. "We can't leave the poor creature here to die."

The puppy looked up at Tara, its huge brown eyes soulful and trusting. "All right, all right," she said. "Put him in the backseat on the floor."

Hope set the puppy down on the floor, and Tara tried not to wince as the animal promptly jumped up onto the backseat.

This is what comes of trying to be nice, Tara lectured herself. First you do Hope a favor by letting her drive. Then one good deed leads to another, and pretty soon your beautiful car is a mess. She was so distracted by her thoughts that she hardly noticed that Hope was having trouble getting the car started.

"I don't know what's wrong," Hope said helplessly as she listened to the motor cough feebly and then die.

"You've probably flooded it," Tara said accusingly.

"I *did not*," Hope contradicted her.

"Now what?" asked Tara. "We're stuck here on this lonely road and it's going to be dark soon. Nice going, Hope."

"Oh, don't be so negative! We'll just get help, that's all."

At that moment, a very large motorcycle pulled into view and Hope got out of the car and waved at it frantically. The cyclist went on by. Tara breathed a sigh of relief. "Do you know who that was you almost flagged down?" she asked Hope. "That was Tony Pell. The one everyone calls 'Tough Tony.' And they're not kidding! Remember? He got kicked out of school last year for stealing a car."

"I don't remember him," admitted Hope. She checked her rearview mirror a bit anxiously. "But it looks like I'm going to meet him now."

Sure enough, Tony Pell had turned around and come back to the pull-off. He stopped his cycle on the shoulder near their parking spot and

15

removed his helmet, revealing a mop of wavy black hair. As he approached the Chevy, Hope became aware that Tony also had the most gorgeous blue eyes she'd ever seen on a boy.

"Well, he certainly doesn't look tough," Hope commented. "In fact, he's kind of cute."

"Cute but dangerous," Tara warned.

Hope, however, was already out of the car, explaining their problem to him. Without so much as a glance in Tara's direction, Tony lifted the hood and began fiddling with the carburetor. When he gave the signal, Hope turned on the ignition again. The car started immediately.

"You'll be all right for now," Tony told them. "But this baby could use a tune-up. It's a shame to have a nice vehicle like this and not maintain it. People are careless with their cars."

You should know, thought Tara. Then Tony's blue eyes fastened on Tara with a look that made her uncomfortably sure he had read her mind.

At that moment, the puppy in the backseat let out a series of high-pitched whimpers. Hope reached back to pet it, and started explaining to Tony how she'd seen it wandering around the pull-off.

"It could be lost," Tony agreed. "But it might have just been abandoned. People dump their dogs here because there's no one around to see them. I guess they hope some kind-hearted person like you will come along and pick them up."

"I don't even know what we're going to do with the poor thing," Hope said. "I can't take it home. My mother is allergic to dogs."

"What do you mean, *we* don't know what we're going to do with it?" Tara exploded. "It was your idea to pick this dog up in the first place. I hope you don't think I'm going to take care of it! My mother would never let me bring a dog in the house to sit on her white couch. I'm lucky she lets me sit on it!"

Hope looked uncertain. "I don't know. Maybe we could take it to the police station. . . ."

Tony laughed so hard that he had to lean against the car to keep from doubling over. "There's an animal shelter in Connorsville," he said, once he'd managed to compose himself. "But they'd probably be closed for the night by the time you got there. Anyway, those places usually have so many dogs that they can't find homes for them all. Especially not for mutts like this. People want purebreds."

Tara was getting impatient. "Let's make up our minds," she told Hope. "I've got to get home."

Hope had opened the back window and Tony was leaning in, scratching the puppy's ears affectionately. "Tell you what," he said. "I live in the country, and one more pet around the house more or less isn't going to make a whole lot of difference. I could keep it for a few days until you girls decide what you want to do with it."

"Would you really? That would be great!" said Hope.

Tony looked at Tara.

"Sure." She shrugged. "That's fine. It isn't my dog to begin with."

Tony cradled the puppy next to his flannel

work shirt and then zipped his leather jacket up part way so that just the dog's snout and ears stuck out. "Come on, Muttsy," he said. "Ready for your first cycle ride?"

"Woof!" The puppy's bark was the first happy sound it had made since they found it.

"See," Tony said. "He knows his name already."

Tony had already revved up his cycle when Hope called out to him. "Wait a second," she said. "How can I get in touch with you?"

"No problem," said Tony. "We're the only Pells in the book."

After he left, Hope put the car in gear and headed back toward Tarenton. "I'm sorry about your backseat getting all dirty," she said after a while.

"That's okay. It's no big deal." Tara looked at Hope warily. "You're not really thinking about calling him up, are you?"

"Of course. I can't just foist that dog off on him. After all, it is my responsibility."

Tara shook her head. "I think you've got a problem with that word. I really do. But take my advice and don't have any more to do with Tony Pell than absolutely necessary. He's bad news."

Hope smiled serenely. "Aren't you being just a little bit melodramatic? After all, he did us a favor. And look how sweet he was with Muttsy."

"I give up," said Tara. "I was just trying to warn you for your own good. But if you don't want to listen to me, fine. What can I do?"

On the way back to town, Tara promised herself again that she was going to stop playing girl scout. That their driving lesson had led to Hope picking up the lost puppy was bad enough, but she would never forgive herself if sweet little Hope got mixed up with Tony Pell.

CHAPTER

In homeroom the next morning, there was a message summoning Olivia to the principal's office.

Uh-oh! she told herself. This could only mean bad news about Coach Engborg. What if she were seriously hurt? What if she were out for the rest of the year?

She knew it was selfish to be worrying about cheerleading at a time like this. The coach's health was far more important. Still, she had to admit feeling frustrated and resentful. Why did the coach have to start showing off and get herself hurt? And just when things were going so well for the squad!

When she got to the administration office, the door to Mrs. Oetjen's private sanctum was closed. Ms. Hanley, the secretary, glanced her way and pushed a letter across the counter. "You're supposed to read this before you go in," she said.

With trembling hands, Olivia tore open the envelope. Inside was a note, in the coach's familiar spiky handwriting:

Dear Olivia,

As you know, the last time I threw out my trick knee, the doctor insisted on surgery. I opted for the minimal surgery, rather than the more extensive operation she recommended. As you see, it didn't work, and I am going to have to have a new operation. This is the same operation they do for professional football players, and when it's over, my knee will be in better shape than it's been in for years. I'm just sorry about the timing.

I'll only be in the hospital for a few days. But when I get out, I won't be very active for a while.

I'm sure you're wondering what this means for the squad.

For some time now, I've been planning to hire an assistant. I had planned to break her in gradually. But now I'm afraid she is going to have to plunge right into the job.

I know you and the others will do everything possible to make her job easier. . . .

The letter went on for a few more paragraphs. Olivia had already started reading ahead, looking for the part that told the new coach's name, when the door to Mrs. Oetjen's office swung open.

"Oh, there you are Olivia," said the principal. "I see you already got Coach Engborg's note. What do you think of our plan?"

"Well. . . ."

She was about to say that she still wasn't sure what the plan was, when a familiar face appeared behind Mrs. Oetjen's.

"Mary Ellen!" Olivia gasped. "What are you doing in school?"

"Didn't you guess? I'm your new assistant coach."

"You're kidding! That's great!"

It seemed too good to be true. Mary Ellen Kirkwood — Olivia's good friend, last year's captain, and everybody's ideal of the perfect cheerleader — was going to be back with the squad.

Of course, Mary Ellen was Mrs. Pres Tilford now. Dressed in a high-fashion navy blue suit, and with her blonde hair done in a sophisticated, up-swept style, she looked very grown-up.

Even so, it took all of Olivia's self-control to keep from jumping up and down and hugging Mary Ellen right there in front of Mrs. Oetjen. She managed to stop herself because she was pretty sure that this wasn't the way to greet a new coach.

But as soon as the two of them left the office and were alone in the hall, Olivia's composure deserted her. "Melon!" she cried. "This is terrific! How come you didn't call me right away and tell me all about it?"

Mary Ellen looked sheepish. "I promised not to say anything. Coach Engborg has been talking to me about the job for weeks. If you ask me, it's all part of a secret plan she has to talk me into becoming a phys. ed. teacher."

"Whatever the reason, I'm just glad we're together again. It's going to be just like old times."

"It sure is!" Mary Ellen agreed. "But let's be a little bit careful in front of Mrs. Oetjen," she added. "I had a tough time convincing her that I could handle running practice while the coach is out sick. Even so, Mrs. Oetjen is going to be hanging around to keep an eye on us. You can't have a school activity meeting without a faculty sponsor, so she's going to be it for the next few days."

"No problem. I figured that out already," Olivia assured her. "Don't worry. We'll treat you just as if you were a real coach — not one of us."

Olivia went back to her first period English class, but it was impossible to concentrate on the teacher's lecture on *Hamlet*.

As soon as the bell rang, she wanted to race around the halls telling the other squad members the news. Then it occurred to her that it might be more fun to make a dramatic announcement at lunchtime, when she could tell the whole group at once.

In between classes that morning, Olivia spread the news that she wanted to have a brief meeting in the cafeteria. Everyone was eager to hear about the coach's condition, and when Olivia arrived, the group was already assembled at their usual table.

Right away, Olivia assured them that Coach Engborg was doing well and would be back in school soon. "And the best part is," she beamed, "we won't miss a single game or practice, because the coach has found the ideal substitute."

Olivia looked around the table at the circle of expectant faces. "You'll never guess who it is," she said.

Tara looked exasperated. "Okay. We give up, so why don't you just tell us?"

"Tara's right," said Sean. "Who could it be? Mary Lou Retton? The president of the International Cheerleading Federation? There aren't all that many exciting possibilities, actually."

"That's what you think," Olivia told him. "You'll change your mind when you hear the name. It's . . . Mary Ellen!"

To her amazement, the announcement was greeted by a wall of silence.

"You're kidding!" Jessica finally managed to gasp. But her tone of voice showed that she was anything but overjoyed.

"Well, I think it's a good idea," said Peter after another long pause.

"What's the matter with the rest of you?" Olivia asked. "We were all at Mary Ellen's wedding. She's practically our best friend."

"Maybe that's part of the problem," said Hope. "It's hard to imagine what it's going to be like having a friend for a coach, even if she is just an assistant."

Olivia felt hurt and rejected. Last year, when she was the only junior on the Varsity Squad, Mary Ellen had been a big help to her. In some ways, she still felt closer to Mary Ellen and her other friends from last year's cheerleading squad than to this year's squad. If everyone felt this cool toward Mary Ellen, maybe they weren't so crazy about her, either.

"I don't know what's wrong with all of you," Olivia said, "but I, for one, think this is the best thing that's happened all year."

After Olivia left the table in a huff, the others sat around sharing an uneasy silence.

Jessica was thinking about Patrick Henley, her current boyfriend and Mary Ellen's old flame. Even though Mary Ellen was married to Pres now, and Patrick was so completely over his crush that he could laugh about it, Jessica wasn't sure she was going to like having Patrick's former girl friend as a coach.

Tara felt pretty much the same way. Mary Ellen was the girl who had everything: gorgeous long blonde hair, a perfect figure, natural leadership ability. Even adults agreed that Mary Ellen was just about perfect: hard-working, unspoiled, and trustworthy.

As far as Tara could see, the closest Mary Ellen had ever come to having a problem was that her family had no money and lived in a small house in a modest part of town. But Mary Ellen had turned even that into an advantage by going off to New York to work as a model and then coming back to marry Pres Tilford, the son of the owner of Tarenton Fabricators. Mary Ellen was Tarenton's Cinderella.

Everyone loves Cinderella, thought Tara. But that's because in the story she goes off with her prince and lives happily ever after. She doesn't hang around, reminding everyone that they'll never be quite as perfect as she is.

Sean Dubrow was almost as disconcerted as the girls. "It certainly is going to be hard getting used to having Mary Ellen as an authority figure," he said.

"I think it can work," insisted Peter. "But I'm a little bit surprised that Olivia is so happy. If I were captain, I'm not sure I'd want to have my predecessor around, second-guessing every move I made."

Peter turned to Hope. "Don't you think so?" he asked.

Hope didn't answer. She was picking at her tuna salad sandwich, her mind a million miles away.

"Earth calling Hope. Come in, Hope," Peter joked.

She looked up, startled. "What?"

"Don't tell me you're brooding about your driver's test again!" Tara said.

"Not really. . . ."

But Tara was already giving the group a dramatic account of the previous day's driving lesson. "There we were, *helpless*," Tara emphasized, "and guess who came along? Tough Tony Pell! I nearly died!"

"He helped us," Hope snapped. "I don't think it's very nice to make fun of him."

Tara ignored her. "The really weird part of the story," she told the others, "is that I think Tony liked Hope. You should have seen the way he was looking at her — all gooey-eyed. He was almost as bad as the puppy."

"What's weird about that?" said Sean. "You're

just jealous because he wasn't paying attention to you."

Tara shook back her long auburn hair. "Well, you would think that I'd be more his type!"

"I'm not sure that's anything to brag about," Peter pointed out. "I remember when Tony Pell left Tarenton High. He'd scratched his initials on the engine block of a stolen car. Talk about major league dumb! Later, the police found the car, and they were going all over town looking for a mechanic with the initials 'TP.' It didn't take them long to find him."

"What happened then?" asked Hope. "Did he get sent to reform school?"

Peter shrugged. "I don't think so. Who knows? All I remember is that he dropped out of school."

"Tony was always a loner, even in grade school," Sean said. "His family lives in that run-down farmhouse out on Route 12, the one with all the old wrecks in the front yard."

"That's right," added Jessica. "His older brother was in the same class as my brother John. All the Pell boys were troublemakers."

Hope had heard enough. "Just listen to yourselves!" she complained. "It seems to me that he never had a chance. You all expected him to turn out badly, and now you seem almost happy that he lived up to your expectations. How smug can you get?"

With that outburst, Hope picked up her tray and marched off. The rest of the group stared in amazement.

"Well, *excuse* me," said Jessica, making a face.

27

"Don't pay any attention to her," said Peter. "Hope means well; she's just a little bit naive."

Jessica didn't feel quite so forgiving. She considered herself a fair person, and didn't appreciate Hope accusing her of being a snob. She was thinking about catching up with Hope so they could talk out the misunderstanding then and there, but she was distracted by the arrival of Diana Tucker.

As usual, Diana's arrival brought all conversation at the cheerleaders' table to a complete stop. Diana always dressed to get attention, but today she had outdone herself. She was wearing a striped turtleneck, along with a clinging jersey skirt.

There was something odd about the skirt, but the group had to study it for quite a while before it dawned on them that it was really just another turtleneck — very oversized, and pulled down around Diana's tiny waist so that the neck became the waistband. The arms were crossed in the front, so that at first glance they looked like the ends of a tie belt.

"What happened?" asked Sean. "Did you get dressed in the dark this morning?"

Diana looked down at her "skirt." "Nothing happened," she said disdainfully. "It's the latest fashion."

Tara couldn't help being impressed. No one would ever catch *her* dressed like that, latest fashion or not. But she did feel envious. Diana did so many outrageous things that she wore people down. Even her teachers tended to overlook Diana's behavior because she was always testing to see how far she could go, and they couldn't react every time.

Although no one had invited her, Diana plunked her tray down at the table, and took a seat between Sean and Peter. "So how do you feel about the Mary Ellen situation?" she asked confidentially. "The news is all over the school."

"I bet," said Jessica. "Now that you know, it would have to be."

Diana smiled, indicating that she had decided to take this as a compliment. "What everyone is wondering," she confided, "is whether you guys are worried. With Mary Ellen around, everyone is bound to compare this year's squad to last year's. More than they already do, I mean."

Peter Rayman was seething. "Are you saying that the kids think last year's squad was better?"

Diana waved her plum-colored fingernails. "I didn't exactly *say* that."

Everyone started talking at once except for Tara, who decided that she wasn't going to let Diana spoil her lunch. Diana's tactics were so obvious that she could hardly believe the others would fall for them.

But they did, every time.

CHAPTER

Hope Chang sat in the chair at the Hair Concept Salon and studied her image in the mirror. "Don't you think I ought to change my hairstyle?" she asked. "I want a cut that says something about the kind of person I am."

Tricia Norris almost dropped her scissors. She had been cutting Hope's hair for almost two years, always in the same simple blunt-cut style. "I think a classic cut is right for you," she said. "If you change it, the only thing your hair is going to say about you is that you're a person who made a mistake at the hair salon."

"Okay. Do what you think best."

Hope hated herself as soon as the words were out of her mouth. She even let herself be bullied by her beautician! Hope-*less*, that's me, she thought. Hope the hopeless.

No wonder Tara thought it was strange that Tony had noticed her.

Or had he noticed her?

Thinking back, Hope wasn't sure that Tara was right about that. Tony had seemed more interested in the puppy than in her. He was really fond of it, she could tell. It was hard to imagine that anyone that soft-hearted about a lost dog could be really bad.

Hope had put an ad about the puppy in the lost and found section of the *Tarenton Lighter* that morning. She didn't have much hope that anyone would answer it, though, and she knew she ought to call Tony soon and ask him if he could keep Muttsy a little longer.

Maybe she would make the call that evening, as soon as she got home.

Tap-tap-tap.

Someone was rapping gently on the glass picture window that looked out onto the enclosed walkway of the Pineland Mall. Hope looked up. It was Tony, dressed in his scruffy leather motorcycle jacket and frayed jeans.

Tricia Norris frowned. "I wish these hoods would leave us alone."

"He's not a hood!" Hope felt the blood rush to her face. "I mean, he's a friend of mine."

As quickly as possible, she paid for her haircut and went out to where Tony was waiting. "This is a crazy coincidence," she said. "I was just thinking about you."

"You were?" Tony looked pleased.

Hope tried not to stare at Tony's eyes, but it was almost impossible not to. He had the longest, curliest lashes she had ever seen on a boy, and they drew attention to the contrast between his

31

dark hair and intense blue eyes. If he ever cleaned up and put on good clothes, he would be really handsome, she thought.

Hope explained about the ad in the paper.

"That's all right. I'm in no hurry to get rid of Muttsy," Tony said. "You should see how nice he looks, all spruced up."

"I'd love to," said Hope, not really thinking about Muttsy.

"The thing is, I have him at the garage where I work sometimes. I'd take you over there to see him, but I just have my cycle, and you wouldn't want to ride on that."

"Actually," said Hope, "I would love to."

Tony brightened. "Then what are we standing around here for? Let's go."

Hope had never ridden on a motorcycle before. At first she was a little bit nervous. Was there anything special she should do? What if she didn't know how to keep her balance? She didn't want to ask questions because she felt embarrassed to admit to Tony that she was a first-time rider.

Tony handed her his extra helmet and then checked carefully to make sure she had it strapped on properly. Doing her best to act blasé, she hopped onto the cycle behind Tony and put her arms around him.

"Hang on tight!" he said.

The motor started with a loud *vroom*, and Hope instinctively clasped her arms around Tony's torso. Any shyness she felt was forgotten as the huge machine dipped sideways to negotiate the spiral ramp out of the parking garage.

Once they turned out onto the main highway, she started to enjoy herself. It was an exciting feeling to be flying down the road without anything between her and the fresh air. Hope started to feel sorry for the drivers who were stuck inside their big, unwieldy cars. They didn't know what they were missing!

The only bad part was the brisk air, but in a way, even that added to the excitement. Fortunately, it was a warm afternoon by Tarenton standards, and Tony's broad shoulders shielded her from the worst of the chill.

They headed back toward Tarenton and then turned off into a section of town near the Tarenton Fabricators factory. The area was mostly warehouses, and the streets were deserted even though it was not yet five o'clock. Hope was just starting to wonder where they were headed, when Tony turned a corner and pulled to a stop.

A half dozen cycles, most of them even bigger and fancier than Tony's, were parked in front of a closed garage door of corrugated metal. Next door there was a bar, one of those dingy places that looks as if the windows hadn't been washed since the day it had opened. The garage itself had no sign on it at all.

Tony pushed open a fire door near the main entrance, and Hope followed him inside. The garage area was an enormous space, filled with motorcycles and cars in various stages of repair. In the back of the room six men, mostly in their early twenties, were sitting around a table, playing cards. When Tony introduced Hope, they looked up from their game just long enough to nod in her direction.

"Muttsy's around here somewhere," said Tony. "I'll go find him."

He disappeared, and Hope stood around trying not to look as out of place as she felt. She couldn't help wondering if this was the place where Tony had scratched his initials on the stolen car. And were the men playing cards a ring of car thieves?

"Here he is."

Tony had returned carrying Muttsy in his arms. In spite of the grease and dirt in the garage, Muttsy was so clean and shining that Hope almost didn't recognize him. The puppy's fur, which had looked so brown and stringy before, was now a soft, reddish gold.

"The vet said he's probably part golden retriever," Tony said.

"You took him to a vet?"

Tony looked embarrassed. "Yeah. He was shaking so much that I thought there must be something wrong with him. But the vet said he was just scared. He needed a little time to understand that he was among friends."

Muttsy had certainly figured that out. As Hope reached out to pet him, he licked her hand eagerly.

For a few minutes, they played with the puppy in silence.

Hope sensed that Tony didn't quite know how to get a conversation started. The feeling was mutual. "Do you really work here?" she asked finally.

Tony shrugged. "Sometimes. Sometimes I just hang around."

"Don't you go to school?"

"Sure," he said. "I go to the vocational high school in Connorsville. It's a waste of time."

"Oh." Tony's reponse left no doubt that he had nothing more to say on the subject of his education. Hope struggled to think of another topic. "I guess you must be good at fixing cars," she said.

Tony's blue eyes seemed to look right through her. "I am. But that's not what you really want to ask, is it? I know what you must have heard about me from your red-headed girl friend. Don't you want to know if it's true?"

Hope hated being put on the spot. "That's all right," she said quickly. "It doesn't matter."

Tony laughed sarcastically. "Of course it matters. You certainly are polite." He made it sound like something to be ashamed of.

"That's more than I can say for you," Hope shot back.

"I'm sorry. It's just hard knowing that everyone I meet thinks I'm a thief. I didn't know that car was stolen. Honest. Otherwise I never would have been dumb enough to put my initials on the engine. That's something I do when I've modified a car for drag racing. It's like an artist signing his name to a painting. But I wouldn't have done that if I were trying to get away with stealing it."

"But the police didn't believe that?" Hope asked.

"They believed it. The charges were dismissed. But by that time, my classmates at Tarenton High had already convicted me. Everyone assumed I was guilty and had just gotten off on some sort of technicality. So I decided never to go back there. Why should I waste my time?"

"But that's terrible!" Hope exclaimed.

Tony suddenly seemed bored with the subject. "Forget it," he said. "I'm probably better off at Connorsville."

He returned Muttsy to the old sofa cushion in the corner that he was using as the puppy's bed. "I'll give you a ride back home now," he said. "I don't suppose you'd want to stop off for a slice of pizza on the way? That is, if you're not worried about being seen with me."

Truthfully, Hope was a little worried. Tony had such a bad reputation that her friends at school would be shocked to see her with him. She was especially worried about what the rest of the squad would think. Coach Engborg was constantly telling them that they had a responsibility to uphold the school's image. It wasn't enough just to stay out of trouble. Cheerleaders represented the school, even when they were out of uniform. And they should avoid doing anything that would give people a bad impression about Tarenton High.

On the other hand, thought Hope, if I say no, I'll be just as bad as all the kids who condemned Tony on hearsay. Rejecting someone without hearing his side of the story isn't right, either.

Besides, it might not be a bad idea to shake up her friends a little bit. She was getting awfully tired of being quiet, reliable, hard-working Hope.

Everyone seemed to have more fun than she did. From now on, she was going to change that.

"I'm not worried," she assured Tony. "Just promise me one thing."

"What's that?" he asked, looking wary.

"Let's order anchovies. I love them, and no one I know does."

He grinned. "It's a deal."

CHAPTER

5

On a normal week night, chances were good that Hope could show up at the Pizza Palace with Tony and not run into more than three or four of her classmates. But this was not an ordinary week night. It seemed as if everyone in town had simultaneously developed a sudden urge for pizza. Maybe this had something to do with the fact that the Pizza Palace was one of Pres Tilford's favorite hangouts. Even now that he and Mary Ellen were married, they often stopped in around dinnertime to get a take-out pie. The news that Mary Ellen was coming back to help coach the cheerleaders had spread all through the school in no time at all, and the Pizza Palace was the obvious place to go to discuss it. With luck, Mary Ellen herself might show up to fill her friends in on the details.

Peter, Tara, Jessica, and Patrick Henley had stopped off there on their way back from Haven

Lake Medical Center, where Patrick had taken them to visit Coach Engborg.

Sean and Kate Harmon dropped by after they finished their volunteer work at the Tarenton Elementary School Sports Clinic, where they helped out with recreational programs for elementary school kids.

Olivia and Duffy were on their way to attend a junior indoor tennis match at Grove Lake, part of a tournament that Duffy was writing up for the sports section of the *Tarenton Lighter*.

Diana Tucker was on hand, too. She and her clique of hangers-on had taken over one of the large tables near the counter where they were sure to see and be seen. Every once in a while, Diana's voice could be heard cutting through the general din of noise and laughter as she told a long, involved story about a beach party she had attended back in California. Diana had transferred to Tarenton High earlier in the year, and she never tired of reminding people what a comedown that had been for her. According to Diana, her life in California had been wildly glamorous and sophisticated. Nothing in Tarenton was quite up to her standards.

"Did it ever occur to you," Duffy said to the cheerleaders, "that someday Diana's family will move to Boston or Texas or somewhere? And then she'll be bragging to everyone there about how popular she was at Tarenton High."

"It can't happen too soon to suit me," sighed Olivia.

"I'll second that," said Jessica. "But it's hard to imagine that even Diana could make Tarenton

39

sound glamorous. Nothing unusual ever happens here. It's just a typical, dull, small town."

"How can you say that?" Tara gasped. "I think Tarenton is beautiful. We have Narrow Brook Lake. We have beautiful scenery. We have the wonderful changes in seasons."

"We sure do have that," laughed Patrick. "Although we've been getting a break lately." He looked out the window where Tony's motorcycle was just pulling into one of the few empty spaces near the front of the restaurant. "Even so, it's a little windy to be tooling around on a motorcycle. You'd have to be a fanatic to want to do that."

Tara laughed. "I seem to remember that you used to be out on your bike on some pretty windy days. Much worse than this. You're just getting old, Patrick Henley."

"Just wait till you turn nineteen, Tara," Patrick joked. "We'll be sure to remind you of that comment. Won't we, Jessica?"

Jessica didn't hear him. She was staring out the window at the parking lot. "I can't believe it!" she exclaimed. "Do you all see what I see? Look who's with Tony Pell!"

Tony saw the reaction their arrival was causing and was not pleased. "Don't expect me to sit with your cheerleader friends," he announced as they went inside. "They have no use for me, and I don't much like them."

So Hope nodded to the group and followed Tony to a table for two across the room. While they ate their pizza, Hope tried to convince Tony that he was being unreasonable. "I think you're

40

being unfair to my friends," she said quietly. "Why not give them a chance?"

Tony was weakening. He had decided long ago that he wanted nothing to do with the Tarenton High in-crowd. They didn't think much of him. So why not reject them before they rejected him? But Hope Chang had him completely confused. He would never have expected a pretty, popular girl like her to waste time talking to him. Yet she wasn't the least bit snooty or stuck up. Amazingly enough, she seemed to like him. And maybe she was right in thinking that anyone she liked would automatically be accepted by her friends.

Aloud, he said, "Okay, Hope. We'll sit with your friends if you want."

He was about to stand up, when Diana Tucker's loud voice cut through the buzz of conversation. "Hope Chang is really slumming," she was saying. "Or maybe we've been wrong about Hope all along. Wouldn't it be a scream if all the time that she was pretending to be Ms. Goody Two-Shoes, she was running around with a motorcycle gang on the sly?"

Tony's blue eyes froze in an icy glare. Before Hope could stop him, he strode over to Diana's table. "Say what you want about me," he announced, "but leave Hope out of this. You have no right to insult her."

Diana was on the verge of making another remark. Then she saw the look on Tony's face and decided, for once, to keep quiet. But Bill Hadley, the Tarenton High basketball player who sometimes dated Diana, wasn't about to let an outsider get away with telling her off.

"She wasn't talking to you," Bill said, coming over from the across the room. "Why don't you mind your own business?"

Tony swung around to face Bill, but since the basketball player was almost a foot taller, he ended up staring into his chest. "I could say the same to you, buddy," he said.

Tony had spoken up on impulse. He hadn't meant to start a fight, and now all he wanted to do was get away before the situation got out of hand.

But Bill Hadley had other ideas. "You're not leaving until you apologize to Diana," he said, grabbing Tony by the elbow.

"Fine," said Tony evenly. "But in that case, I think she ought to apologize to Hope."

"I don't care what you think," retorted Bill, tightening his grip on Tony's arm.

Tony glowered. "Let go of me, or else."

Diana put her hands to her face and squealed, half in fear and half in delight that Bill Hadley was actually about to get into a fight on her behalf.

At the cheerleaders' table, everyone was watching in dismay. Finally, Sean and Peter exchanged glances and nodded. By silent agreement they got up and went to separate Tony and Bill.

"We don't need any fighting in here," said Sean quietly.

To his relief, Tony shrugged and retreated back to his own table. "Come on, Hope," he said. "Let's get out of here."

Hope looked mortified, but she gathered up her belongings and followed Tony out of the restaurant. Diana watched her go, with a look of smug satisfaction spread across her face. "Imagine that!" she said, when Tony was safely out the door. "Hope Chang and the local hood. That's an odd couple if I ever saw one!"

"You two shouldn't have interfered," Diana added, turning to Sean and Peter. "You should have let Bill teach him a lesson."

"Right," mumbled Bill Hadley, without much conviction.

"They shouldn't let troublemakers like him come in here," Diana added.

"If they didn't," Peter told her, "you would be eating your pizza in the parking lot."

Peter didn't wait to hear Diana's reaction. He wasn't sure at the moment with whom he was angrier. Diana was a loudmouth. But Hope Chang was almost worse. He didn't mind any more that he and Hope had decided to stop dating. Still, it hurt to think that Tony Pell was taking his place. Although he would never admit it to anyone, he often felt that girls would like him better if he weren't so easygoing. Girls seemed to be more attracted to the macho, muscleman type. Even Hope, who was so sweet and quiet!

Glumly, Peter returned to the cheerleaders' table, where Duffy was trying to smooth over the situation with humor. "I would have helped you guys out," he told Sean and Peter, "but I didn't want to overwhelm those two with a show of brute force. Besides, it's against my religion to fight. I'm a devout pacifist."

For once, Duffy's jokes were having no effect.

Peter sat toying with his slice of pizza for a while, then stood up. "I think I'll walk home," he announced. "I could use some fresh air."

"Well," said Jessica, as soon as he was gone, "I can see why Peter is upset, but I guess Hope has a right to go out with whomever she wants to."

"But what about us?" asked Olivia. "I'm not just thinking of the squad. I thought we were Hope's best friends. Why would she want to date someone who won't even say hello to us? Besides, you know what kind of reputation Tony Pell has!"

"I warned Hope about him," Tara reminded everyone. "I don't understand how she can do this to us."

Olivia sighed. "Me, neither. I don't think we should discuss it now, though. Let's wait and see what happens."

Everyone tried to change the subject, but trying not to talk about Hope and Tony was hard work. Besides, it was becoming obvious that Mary Ellen and Pres were not going to show up that evening. Soon Olivia and Duffy departed, followed by Tara and Jessica.

When everyone else was gone, Sean looked fondly across the table at Kate Harmon. He couldn't help suspecting that Olivia's reason for not wanting to discuss Hope had to do with Kate's presence. The others liked her. But she was definitely an outsider.

Sean knew that most of the guys in his class couldn't understand why he was dating Kate. To his eyes, Kate's frizzy brown hair and freckled complexion were beautiful. But Kate was not the

44

sort of knockout beauty that everyone expected to see on the arm of Sean Dubrow. Kate didn't wear makeup, and her interest in clothes was nil. More important, she had strong opinions and a disconcerting way of saying exactly what was on her mind.

Some guys might have found Kate's direct manner too much to deal with, but not Sean. Tall, broad-shouldered, and handsome, Sean was used to thinking that he could date any girl he wanted. When he first realized that Kate was not exaclty bowled over by his dazzling charms, he had been annoyed, then intrigued. After a while, he began to realize that he felt more comfortable and happy with Kate than he ever had with any other girl. It was good to know that Kate wasn't going out with him because she wanted to make an impression on her girl friends.

So far, the girls on the cheerleading squad had gone out of their way to be nice to Kate. But Sean could tell that even they were a little bit leery. After all, Kate attended a rival school. That took some getting used to for his teammates. But Kate thought of them as friends, not rivals. It would just take time for the others to figure that out.

At the moment, Sean had no patience for trying to bridge the gap between Kate and his friends. He wanted her all to himself. "Let's go over to my house," he suggested to her. "I've got some new tapes I want you to hear."

To his surprise, Kate shook her head. "I really should be getting home. I've got a French assignment to do."

"I thought you were up late last night studying French," he said. "Your teacher must be a real slave driver."

Kate looked embarrassed. "You caught me," she admitted. "It's true. My French assignment is done. I was just making an excuse."

Sean felt the muscles in his neck tighten. The pizza in his stomach seemed to be settling into an indigestible lump. Other girls might make up excuses for trivial reasons, but not Kate.

Suddenly, it occurred to him that Kate hadn't been to his house for some time now. Was something wrong?

"What's the matter?" he asked aloud. "Don't you want to be alone with me?" He had meant the question to be a joke, but there was no disguising the hurt and anxiety he felt.

Kate squeezed his hand. "Are you crazy?" she asked. "Of course I do. It's my folks who aren't wild about the idea. You can come to my place if you want. But. . . ."

"But *what*?"

Kate bit her lip nervously. "But they don't want me to spend too much time at your house. They didn't exactly forbid me to come over. But it's become an issue. Let's just be cool for a while, and I'm sure they'll forget all about it. Okay?"

Sean wanted to take Kate's advice, but he felt hurt and indignant. "What's wrong with my house?" he demanded. "Isn't it fancy enough for their daughter?"

"That's unfair and you know it!" Kate retorted, her expressive eyes blazing with indignation. "It's just that your dad is never home. That's all."

"And they don't trust us! Right?"

"They trust us," Kate assured him. "Don't be so touchy. But it doesn't look good. You know how people talk."

"I sure do!"

Sean's father had a reputation around town as something of a ladies' man. In a big city, there would have been nothing remarkable about Mark Dubrow. But Tarenton did not have that many single fathers, at least not young-looking, fun-loving ones like him. At one time or another, Mr. Dubrow had probably dated half the single women in town. Occasionally, Sean found it awkward to run into a store clerk, an adult fan at a basketball game, or even a teacher, and realize that he had met her already as one of his father's dates. It was always hard to know how to act in situations like that, and Sean invariably said hello, but then pretended that he could not quite recall the details of where they'd run into each other before.

Still, there was nothing wrong with his father going out on dates. Sean was proud of his dad's youthful looks. Mark Dubrow kept himself in peak condition and was probably more fit than most guys still in high school. And it was fun having a father who was also a buddy, who liked the same music he did, and sometimes even wore the same clothes.

Suddenly, Sean felt that if he gave in and went over to the Harmons' house, he would be disloyal to his dad. "I think your folks are out of line," he told Kate. "Anyway, I want to listen to those tapes. If you don't want to come along, fine. I'll drop you at your house."

Kate looked pained. "If that's the way you feel about it," she said, "I guess I have no choice."

When they kissed good-bye in his Fiero parked in the Harmon driveway, Kate looked miserable. "I really am on your side," she told Sean. "But I can't defy my parents over this."

"Yeah, right," he grumbled.

On the drive home, Sean indulged in feeling sorry for himself. Probably Mr. Harmon is just jealous of my old man, he thought.

Sean had to admit that the idea of Mr. Harmon wanting to listen to Cyndi Lauper records or drive a high-performance car was pretty improbable. He was strictly the type who preferred easy-listening music and a sensible Buick sedan. Still, the image was funny enough that he couldn't wait to mention it to his dad. He was already rehearsing how he could turn the Harmons' complaint into an amusing story.

Sean pulled into the garage and let himself into the house through the side door. Lights were on in every room, but his dad didn't answer when he called out. A stack of dirty dishes piled in the sink and some half-spoiled cold cuts left out on the counter reminded him that their housekeeper, known affectionately as Windy, was still away on vacation, visiting her sister.

In the living room he found more evidence of Windy's absence: a pile of newspapers and opened junk mail on the coffee table, topped by two half-empty soda cans.

Sean spent the next hour or so straightening up.

He piled the week's accumulation of newspapers near the fireplace, threw the laundry into the hamper, and straightened up the bedrooms. Then Marge Kopecky, one of the secretaries from his dad's office, called, and Sean had to tell her that he really didn't know when his father was going to be home. That was annoying. Sean liked Marge, and he was afraid she would think Dad was around and just didn't want to talk to her.

"We've got to train the old man better," he groused out loud.

Just then, he heard his father's car pull into the garage. Mr. Dubrow came in, took a can of soda out of the fridge on his way through the kitchen, and settled down in his favorite chair in the living room.

Sean told him about the phone call. "I didn't know what to say to Marge," he added. "I wish you'd leave me a note or something, telling me when you're coming home."

Mr. Dubrow raised one eyebrow. "I'm not used to people keeping tabs on my whereabouts," he said. "Marge will have to get used to that."

Or else she won't, thought Sean, and pretty soon we can add her name to the list of nice women who have given up on Mark Dubrow. Aloud, he said, "If you don't want her to know where you are, I wish you'd at least tell me."

"Good grief!" Mr. Dubrow was shuffling through the pile of newspapers Sean had just stacked up. "You're starting to sound like a nagging parent," he complained. "And you've hidden my newspaper, besides."

"I'm not nagging. . . ."

"I know, son." Mr. Dubrow chuckled. "That was supposed to be a joke. But you'd better watch out, all the same. I think you're getting too serious about that Harmon girl. She's starting to domesticate you."

"Don't criticize Kate," Sean shot back. "This has nothing to do with her."

"Whatever you say." Mr. Dubrow was already engrossed in the business section of the paper and didn't even notice the challenging tone in his son's voice. As far as he was concerned, the discussion was over.

Sean grabbed his new tapes and retreated to his bedroom. With his portable tape deck turned up to full volume, he stretched out on his bed and tried to relax. Maybe his dad was right after all, he told himself. Maybe he *was* starting to get too serious about Kate.

On the other hand, he was also starting to understand why the Harmons didn't want Kate to hang around his house. It wasn't just that the place wasn't neat, or that his father wasn't home a lot of the time. It was. . . .

Sean tried, but he couldn't quite think of a way to put the problem into words. Surely no one could blame his dad because he had never found anyone special enough to replace Mom. Sean had never wanted a stepmother, and in a way he was glad that his father hadn't remarried. But lately he was beginning to wonder what would happen to his father when he went away to college. He couldn't depend on Windy to keep the family together forever. After all, she was only a housekeeper. What if she decided to retire and live with her sister for good? Or got married herself? Or got a new job?

Sean shook his head, put on another tape, and shoved his worries to the back of his mind. There was nothing he could do about the problem tonight, anyway. So he might as well just lie back and listen to the music.

CHAPTER

6

"The Wolves have got the talent,
The Wolves have got the speed!
The Wolves have got the spirit
No one can tame!

The Wolves have got the defense,
The Wolves have got the plays!
The Wolves have got the classy moves,
That's why we'll win the game."

Olivia pumped her arms and jumped as high as she could, and on the last word of the cheer she led the squad in doing a perfectly timed split. It was Mary Ellen's first practice, and Olivia was determined to show her former teammate what this year's squad could do. Perhaps she was showing off a little bit, but she felt she had a right. She was proud of how far she'd come, from last year's insecure junior member to this year's captain.

When the last reverberations of the cheer faded, and Mary Ellen responded by applauding the squad's efforts, Olivia felt as if she would burst with pride. She called for several more fight cheers. And then, when Mary Ellen called them to the bleachers for a conference, she fairly bounded to her friend's side.

"That was wonderful," Mary Ellen told them. "You kids really have it all. I can see that there isn't much that I have to teach you."

Nevertheless, Mary Ellen seemed to have made quite a few notes on the yellow legal pad that was attached to her clipboard. She studied them for a few seconds with a look of intense concentration. "The only suggestion I have at all," she said hesitantly, "is that maybe you're trying to do too much."

Olivia felt as if she'd been slapped. "What do you mean?" she asked.

"Take the 'We've Got the Spirit' cheer, for example," Mary Ellen said. "I wonder if you haven't got too many complicated moves in there."

She set down her clipboard. "I've been attending a special course on cheerleading given by the phys. ed. department at Hillsborough Junior College, and one of the things they stress is that some squads get too carried away with fancy gymnastics. There are a lot of other things you could do to develop a unique style."

"I agree," Hope said.

"We've got that line in the cheer about 'classy moves.' So why don't we work out a routine that starts from there?" Peter suggested.

"You sound as if you have some ideas," Mary Ellen said.

A bit shyly at first, Peter demonstrated what he had in mind. His version of the cheer left out two jumps and the split at the end, but added a strutting dance step and a few high kicks.

Olivia frowned. There was no question that Peter was a good dancer. When he did those moves, they looked great. But that was exactly the problem, as far as she was concerned. Peter's moves were so much his own that she didn't see how the rest of the squad could execute them without looking like a bunch of Peter Rayman clones.

"I don't know . . ." Olivia said aloud.

"I think it's fantastic," Mary Ellen exclaimed. "That's exactly what I meant by a unique style. If you reworked more of your routines around those moves, you wouldn't look like any other cheerleading squad around."

We wouldn't even look like ourselves, Olivia thought glumly.

But Tara was already trying out Peter's suggestion. "What we really need is some sort of new prop," she said enthusiastically. "Like a baton. Or a cane."

Peter ran into Mrs. Engborg's office and returned with a yardstick. "You mean, like this?" Planting the stick on the floor, he did a soft-shoe shuffle around it.

"Great," said Olivia sarcastically. "Maybe we could have top hats, too. And wear white tie and tails."

"Or like Liza Minelli," Tara said, her eyes

shining. "That would be the *ultimate*. I've always wanted to wear one of those costumes. You know, with the bow tie and long black stockings. . . ."

Jessica nudged Tara with her elbow. "I don't think Olivia meant that seriously," she whispered.

"Oh." Tara looked completely deflated. "Really? But it would be dreamy. . . ."

Mary Ellen tensed. She hadn't meant to start a controversy. Now Olivia would think that she was trying to revamp the squad's entire image. "Well, it's something to think about," she backtracked. "Let's put it aside for now, and go on with practice."

Olivia breathed a sigh of relief. "Good idea," she said. "Okay, squad. We need to work on our routine for the fight song — the one where I do the dismount from a pyramid."

"Uh-uh." Mary Ellen shook her head. "I'm afraid we'll have to pass up that one. Coach Engborg doesn't want you practicing any pyramids until she comes back."

"But Melon!" Olivia protested. "We've done that routine hundreds of times. We know all the safety precautions. We're going to do it at Saturday's game. Why not during practice?"

"You won't be doing it at Saturday's game, either," Mary Ellen said. "I'm sorry."

"Melon! You can't do this to us!"

Mary Ellen's voice turned icy. "I am not doing anything to you. Those are the *coach's* orders. If you don't like it, you can ask Mrs. Oetjen."

Tarenton High's principal had been seated high up in the bleachers, doing some paperwork while keeping an eye on the practice. At the sound of her name she looked up and smiled. "Did you have a question?" she asked.

"No. That's okay." Olivia said, giving in.

Olivia led the rest of the afternoon's cheers through clenched teeth. Jessica had tried to warn her that Mary Ellen's return might lead to a tense situation, but she hadn't believed her. Who would have thought that her good friend would immediately set out to undermine her leadership of the squad?

Mary Ellen looked equally unhappy. She supervised the rest of the routines in silence, but as soon as the squad headed for the locker rooms, she called Olivia to her side. "I think we have a few things to talk over," she began.

"I don't see what can be left to discuss," Olivia said defiantly.

"Olivia, this is hard for me, too," Mary Ellen told her. "I'm not trying to stir up trouble for you, honest."

"You could have fooled me."

The hurt look on Mary Ellen's face made Olivia relent. She sat down on the bleacher beside her friend. "All right," she said. "Let's talk."

"First of all," Mary Ellen told her, "if you'd been to see Coach Engborg since the accident, she would have explained why you can't do pyramids until she comes back. It's a safety regulation, nothing personal."

"Oh." As much as she hated to admit it, Olivia had to agree that that made sense.

"How come you haven't been to see her?" Mary Ellen asked. "Do you know that you're the only member of the squad who hasn't even called her?"

56

"I meant to," Olivia explained. "I spent so much time in hospitals when I was younger, and every time I went in for another heart operation I was terrified. I suppose I just put off visiting Mrs. Engborg."

But Olivia knew it wasn't the real story. She was putting off visiting the coach because she felt partly responsible for her getting hurt. If only she hadn't let Coach Engborg down by being late for practice, the accident would never have happened.

"I know the coach would like to see you," Mary Ellen said. "She's been thinking about some new ideas, and I know she wants to discuss them with you."

Olivia was immediately suspicious. "What new ideas?"

"I think you should hear them from her," Mary Ellen said uneasily.

"Don't be like that," Olivia pleaded. "You're my friend, too, remember? Can't you at least give me a hint?"

Mary Ellen didn't know what to do. The coach hadn't exactly sworn her to secrecy, and she felt desperate to prove to Olivia that her new job didn't mean the end of their friendship. "Okay," she said. "After she got hurt, the coach started thinking about how it would affect the squad if someone got sick, or had to drop out for some reason. And she came up with this great idea. Alternates!"

"What?!"

"Alternates," Mary Ellen repeated. "She's thinking about holding tryouts and picking a few alternates to attend practice with the Varsity Squad. I think it's a good idea, too. It could be the first step toward expanding the squad."

Olivia could hardly believe her ears. Naming alternates was the worst plan she could imagine. For one thing, it would play right into the hands of that scheming Diana Tucker. Ever since she'd transferred to Tarenton High, Diana had been looking for a way to worm her way into a place on the squad. "I'll tell you one thing," Olivia told the startled Mary Ellen. "If that dumb blonde Diana is allowed to attend practices, I'm quitting."

"Aren't you jumping to conclusions?" Mary Ellen protested. "And what's this about dumb blondes? I know you don't like Diana, but that's just a stereotype."

"Don't be silly, Melon," Olivia cut in. "I didn't mean you."

Mary Ellen understood that, but she had been saddled with the "dumb blonde" image too often herself not to take the phrase personally. Olivia knew her well enough to understand that. Or she should have.

For that matter, she had never been crazy about the nickname Melon, either. And she worried that if Mrs. Oetjen heard Olivia using it during practice, she would get the wrong impression. "I know I'm not an official teacher," Mary Ellen informed Olivia frostily. "So I can't expect you to call me Ms. Tilford. But you could at least try not to address me as 'Melon.' "

For Olivia, that was the last straw. "If that's

the way you want it," she said, and stomped off to the locker room.

Hope Chang had already dressed and gone, but Jessica was combing her hair and Tara was still in her leotard, practicing high kicks in front of the full-length mirror. Tara loved to daydream, and just the mention of a top-hat-and-tails dance routine was enough to set her to fantasizing that she was the star of a sophisticated night club act. She had combed her long auburn mane so that it hung alluringly over one shoulder, and between kicks she was trying out a variety of sultry expressions.

"It's all a big cabaret," she sang as she danced. "Join in our cabaret."

Olivia was in a rotten mood and she was sure that Tara was just trying to razz her. "Stop that! Don't you ever quit?" she snapped.

Astonished, Tara flung her hair back over her shoulder and stared. "Who appointed you dictator?"

"Don't worry," Olivia retorted, "you won't have to put up with me too much longer. Just wait until you have to cheer with Diana Tucker. Then see how you like it!"

Tara flashed Jessica a perplexed look and returned to practicing her kicks, this time in silence.

Jessica couldn't stop herself from laughing. She was actually sympathetic to Olivia, but Tara's bewilderment struck her as hilarious. Somehow, Tara had managed to glide through practice completely oblivious to the tensions vibrating around her. There were certain advantages to being somewhat self-centered.

Unfortunately, Olivia heard Jessica's giggles and wheeled around to confront her. "It's easy for you to laugh at this," she accused, "now that you and Patrick are hanging around with Mary Ellen and Pres all the time. I bet you knew all about this long before I did."

"All about what?" asked Jessica. "I have no idea what you're talking about."

But Jessica was talking to empty air. Olivia had marched into the shower, and she didn't come out until the other girls were long gone.

CHAPTER

In spite of what Olivia thought, Jessica hadn't heard a word about the plan to hold tryouts for alternates. But Olivia's words had struck home for a different reason. As it happened, she and Patrick were double-dating with Pres and Mary Ellen that very evening, and Jessica wasn't at all happy about the arrangement.

For two weeks now, she had been looking forward to seeing a movie version of the ballet *Romeo and Juliet*, which was showing at the College Theater in Hillsborough. Ballet movies weren't exactly Patrick's idea of fun — his tastes ran more to Steve Martin comedies, or thrillers — but he had promised to take Jessica, anyway. Then, two days ago, he had called her up to say that Mary Ellen wanted to see *Romeo and Juliet*, too. Would Jessica mind if the four of them went together?

Jessica agreed because she wanted to be a good

sport. Still, she looked forward to the evening ahead with mixed feelings. She couldn't forget that not so long ago, Patrick had been desperately in love with Mary Ellen. The strange thing was that Patrick himself almost seemed to have forgotten. It wasn't in Patrick's nature to do things halfway. Once he had decided that he no longer loved Mary Ellen, that was it as far as he was concerned. That episode of his life was finished, and he didn't feel the least bit awkward about seeing Mary Ellen as a friend.

Mary Ellen and Pres, meanwhile, were so wrapped up in each other that they thought of everything that happened before their wedding as ancient history.

So that left Jessica as the only member of the foursome who felt ill at ease. She had thought that once Mary Ellen and Pres were married, her jealousy would fade. Instead, it had just mellowed into resentment. There were times when Mary Ellen and Pres exuded so much newlywed bliss that she wanted to scream. And what was worse, Patrick seemed to regard their relationship as the perfect model for him and Jessica to follow.

As she dressed for the movie, Jessica promised herself that she wasn't going to let Mary Ellen's presence spoil her special evening. She made an extra effort to look her best, putting on a new green silk blouse that brought out the green in her eyes, and a pair of camel-colored slacks with double pleats in the front and slightly tapered ankles. At the last minute, she borrowed several of her mother's gold chains and drapped them around her neck to soften the blouse's V-neck.

Studying the effect in her mirror, she was pleased. The slacks emphasized her long legs and tiny waist, and the color combination was just right for her. Her brown hair shimmered with golden highlights.

At six-thirty, Patrick drove up in the van that belonged to H&T's TLC Moving, the company he had started in partnership with Pres. Jessica sighed. She was beginning to see that Patrick was the sort of person who would never drive just an ordinary, utilitarian car. It wasn't a question of money. Vehicles were an extension of his personality, and to drive a car that looked like everyone else's would have made him miserable. For now, one of his trucks suited him fine.

As she got to the van, she saw that Patrick had at least been thoughtful enough to cover the grimy seat with a clean blanket. "You look terrific," he said, flashing her one of his magnetic smiles.

When they got to Pres and Mary Ellen's there was another change of plans. "I'm afraid Mary Ellen forgot that she had promised to watch our neighbor's baby here tonight," Pres explained. "The baby's already asleep, so I thought it would be just as good if we stayed here and watched the movie on our VCR." He held up a cassette. "I had to go all the way to Connorsville to find this, so I hope it's all right, Jessica."

Jessica could see that the movie wasn't the right one at all. It was the Shakespearean play, in a version by some Italian director, not the ballet she had her heart set on seeing. But what could she do? Glancing at her watch, she realized that it was already too late to get to the College Theater in time for the seven o'clock performance. And Pres had gone to so much effort to please her that she didn't want to hurt his feelings by telling him he'd made a mistake.

While Pres and Patrick fussed with the VCR, Mary Ellen showed off the latest additions to the house — a new dishwasher, some shelves Pres had put up in the kitchen, and a new set of dishes, extras passed on to them by Pres's mother. Then the neighbor's baby woke up and started to cry. While Mary Ellen held the infant, Jessica went into the kitchen to warm its bottle. Testing the formula to see if it was warm enough, she managed to spill some of it on her new blouse.

By the time they got around to watching the tape, it was eight-thirty. Jessica sat on the couch with Patrick, trying to pretend that she was having a good time. Her blouse smelled of milk, and although she had tried to clean up the spill right away, there was still a dark, blotchy stain down the front.

Mary Ellen and Pres hadn't been too sure that they would enjoy Shakespeare, but soon they were completely engrossed in the story of the young lovers kept apart by their feuding families.

When Romeo and Juliet committed suicide rather than give each other up, Mary Ellen dissolved into tears. "That's the saddest movie I ever saw," she said with satisfaction as the film ended.

Jessica squirmed. "I thought the ending was silly," she complained. "I'd never commit suicide, no matter what. Besides, why were Romeo and

Juliet in such a rush to get married when they were still teenagers? If I were Juliet, I'd stay single as long as possible."

Pres let out a bark of laughter. "Just wait a few months. You'll soon change your mind about that."

"That's right," said Mary Ellen with a knowing smile. "Last year at this time, I would have said the same thing."

"But I'm not you," Jessica protested. "I wasn't criticizing your choice. I'm just saying that getting married young isn't for everyone."

Pres looked pained. He hated to see other people arguing. "We know that," he said, trying to make peace. "Mary Ellen just meant that people grow up pretty quickly once they get out of high school. You'll see."

Jessica felt her ears reddening with anger and frustration. It was bad enough that her plans for the evening had been ruined, but she hated the feeling that her ideas weren't being taken seriously. "I'm not a child," she snapped. "My opinions are just as good as anyone else's."

"Hey, I didn't mean that you were a child. I'm sorry."

Despite Pres's apology, Jessica felt like a little kid who had just thrown a tantrum. Mary Ellen quickly changed the subject, and Patrick patted her on the shoulder comfortingly and mumbled that it was getting to be time to leave.

In the van on the way home, Patrick didn't know what to say. "What's wrong, Jessica?" he asked anxiously. "Is it something I did?"

But Jessica was too tired to review the disappointments of the evening. When she and Patrick were alone together, everything could seem so right, so perfect. She snuggled closer to his muscular arm. "Forget it," she said. "We'll talk about it some other time."

That night, she dreamed that she and Patrick were getting married. Pres and Mary Ellen were there, too, standing in as best man and matron of honor. At first, Jessica felt happy. Then, gradually, she began to realize that the scene was not right. Instead of being in a church, the wedding was taking place in a department store. There was a row of dishwashers where the altar would have been, and piles of dishes and appliances were standing all around them. Next, she noticed that Mary Ellen was wearing her cheerleading practice clothes and held a whistle in her hand, ready to criticize her every move.

"I'm not ready for this," she heard herself saying.

"Yes, you are," Mary Ellen told her. "Just wait. Last year at this time, I would have said the same thing."

"But I'm not you," she protested. She turned to run away, but her feet felt as if they had heavy weights attached to them. Every step was a struggle, and the more she tried to run, the more she felt Patrick's firm but gentle grip on her arm, pulling her back.

"I'm not Mary Ellen! I'm Jessica!"

When she opened her eyes, she was sitting bolt upright in the darkness. The dream had been so real that she had to switch on her bedside light to prove to herself that she was safe at home, in her own bedroom.

What am I going to do now? she asked herself. She loved Patrick, and she could hardly expect him to stop hanging around with his best friends, especially not since he and Pres had been partners, and Pres still helped out from time to time. Still, she hated being the junior member of the Pres-and-Mary Ellen, Patrick-and-Jessica foursome. There had to be some way to make the others see that.

Sean Dubrow was thinking about marriage that evening, too. But not his own. His father's.

"I have an idea that will solve all our problems," he told Kate. "If my father remarried, then your parents would forget about their objections to your being around my house, right?"

They were sitting in the Harmons' basement recreation room watching television, and Kate was balancing an enormous bowl on her knees. She helped herself to a handful of buttery popcorn and considered the problem.

"I guess not. But how are we going to get your father to cooperate? I haven't seen any signs that your dad is thinking about getting married. Love'em and leave'em, that's his motto."

Sean grinned. "That used to be mine, too. Until I met you. Maybe Dad just needs a little encouragement."

Kate looked skeptical, but Sean began telling her about Marge Kopecky, the secretary in his father's office. Marge's husband had run a small charter flying service until he was killed in a plane crash five years ago. Marge had no children and she lived in a studio apartment, so if she married Mr. Dubrow, she would probably be willing to move into his big house, and Sean's life wouldn't change too drastically.

"Besides," added Sean cheerfully, "Marge has a pilot's license, so if she and Dad got married, I could get free flying lessons."

"Great," said Kate sarcastically. "I'm sure if you just point that out to your father, he'll propose to Marge right away."

But Sean refused to be discouraged. "My father likes Marge," he insisted. "They've dated for a few weeks now. I bet if he had a chance to spend time with her at our home, and to see how well she and I get along, he'd start to think of getting serious. Friday night is Dad's birthday. We could celebrate by cooking dinner and inviting Marge over."

Kate reached for another handful of popcorn. "I don't know about that," she warned. "Matchmaking can backfire."

"I don't see how," Sean insisted. "If it doesn't work, then fine. But what harm can we do?"

Before Kate could think of any more objections, Sean went to the phone and called Mrs. Kopecky. "We're having a little celebration in honor of my father's birthday," he told her. "And we wondered if you would like to come."

Minutes later, he rejoined Kate on the couch. "She seemed a little bit surprised," he reported, "but she said yes. Now all we have to do is figure out the menu. What do you know how to cook?"

Kate pointed to the bowl on her lap. "I'm a whiz at microwave popcorn," she said. "But that's as far as my repertoire goes."

"But I thought all girls knew how to cook something!"

"Think again," Kate told him.

Sean let the news sink in. "Okay," he said, "I'll do the cooking. How hard can it be? Will you at least help?"

"On one condition," said Kate. "I have to plan the program for the sports clinic's open house this Sunday. Can you get the cheerleaders to come? The squad could give a demonstration, then divide the kids into groups and show them a few exercises and cheers. The parents could join in, too, if they wanted to. I've been trying to think of an activity that would get everyone involved, and this will demonstrate that our program is more than just basketball and volleyball."

"Why not?" said Sean. "It'll be good public relations for the squad and it won't take long. Now, let's get back to thinking about that menu."

Kate found several cookbooks in the kitchen, and for the next half hour they skimmed the pages looking for something they felt capable of making. Unfortunately, most of the recipes had mysterious French names, like *cassoulet* and *pot au feu*.

"I can't even pronounce these dishes, much less cook them," Sean complained. "Why don't we just serve something simple, like meat loaf and mashed potatoes? Windy makes that in no time at all, so it can't be too complicated."

Sean set aside the cookbooks and pulled Kate

close. "I just know this is going to work," he predicted. "I'll think of an excuse to keep my father at home, but we'll sort of make the rest of our plans a surprise. I can't wait to see the look on Dad's face when he realizes that we've planned it all just for him."

CHAPTER

Diana Tucker was happily giving her version of Tony Pell's visit to the Pizza Palace to anyone who would listen. "Tony practically assaulted me," she told Holly Hudson in gym class on Thursday morning. "If it weren't for Bill Hadley, I could have been seriously injured."

"But how did the trouble start?" Holly asked.

Diana sniffed. "Personally, I think Hope put him up to it. Hope has been jealous of me ever since I came to Tarenton High and took Peter Rayman away from her."

"That doesn't sound like Hope," Holly objected. "But, then, it isn't like Hope to be involved with Tony, either."

"But she is," Diana insisted. "Ask anyone who was there."

Holly knew from experience that Diana was not a reliable source of information, but she found it hard to resist a juicy tidbit of gossip. So when the Pompon Squad met later that morning, Holly wasted no time in sharing the story with them.

"Did you hear that Hope Chang is going out with Tony Pell, the kid who got arrested last year for stealing cars?" she told everyone. "They were in the Pizza Palace the night before last, and he attacked Diana Tucker for no reason at all. It took three guys to save her."

By lunchtime, the story had been improved still further. According to one version, Hope and Tony were going steady. In another, Hope and Diana had gotten involved in a real fight and Tony had interfered when Diana seemed to be winning. The wildest version of the story was that Hope and Tony were breaking into cars in the parking lot and when Diana caught them, they tried to beat her up.

"I know that isn't true," reported Carla Simpson as she repeated rumor number three to Olivia. "But I just thought you ought to hear what's going around."

"But that's crazy," Olivia said. "No one could possibly believe that."

"Maybe they don't believe all of it," Carla corrected her. "But I bet a lot of kids believe the part about Hope being mixed up with a boy who's been in trouble with the police."

Olivia sighed. She knew that Carla meant well, but she wasn't sure what she was supposed to do about the gossip. Hope's private life was her own business. On the other hand, the trouble at the Pizza Palace had nearly resulted in Sean and Peter getting involved in a fistfight, and if anything like that happened again, it would be a disaster for the squad.

This is just the kind of situation that Mary Ellen would have known how to handle, Olivia told herself. Of course, now that Mary Ellen was around again, she could always ask her for advice. But to do that would be practically an admission that she couldn't handle the responsibility of being captain without help.

As she thought the situation over, Olivia was absentmindedly pushing her tray through the cafeteria serving line. Suddenly, a voice broke through her train of thought. "Do you want the daily special, or not?" it asked impatiently.

"What?" She looked up into the eyes of one of the cafeteria aides, a big, red-faced woman with a voice liked raked gravel.

"What . . . do . . . you . . . want . . . to . . . eat?" the woman asked, forming each word carefully as if she were talking to someone who didn't understand English very well. Two freshman who were behind Olivia in the line snickered.

"I'm sorry," Olivia said. "I don't know what I want. Anything."

"Good." The aide slapped a large helping of pinkish goop onto Olivia's plate. "I've been trying to foist this stuff onto someone all day," she added.

The freshmen snickered again, and Olivia stared down at her tray. The cafeteria's version of lasagna hadn't been very good yesterday when it was freshly made, and it looked even less appetizing today.

At least the inedible lunch would help her

make up her mind. Grabbing an apple on her way out of the serving area, she dumped the lasagna in the trash and headed out of the cafeteria to look for Hope. She found her in the orchestra room, practicing the violin.

"I hate to interrupt," she apologized, "but I need to talk to you."

Hope put down her violin and smiled. "Sure. What's the problem?"

Olivia wasn't quite sure what to say. "I know this is none of my business," she began, "but it's about Tony Pell."

"What about him?"

Haltingly, Olivia repeated the rumors that were going around school. "I know a lot of that isn't true," she summed up. "But there was almost a fight at the Pizza Palace. And you know how upset Coach Engborg would be if any of us got involved in an incident like that."

"You're right," Hope said. "Most of the things the kids say about Tony Pell aren't true. But I'm certainly not planning to do anything that would embarrass the coach, if that's what you're worried about."

Olivia breathed a sigh of relief. "Good. I didn't want to butt in. I really didn't. But I feel better knowing that you aren't planning to go out with Tony again."

Hope stiffened. "I didn't say that."

Up to that moment, Hope really hadn't been planning to see Tony again. Although she didn't think the trouble at the Pizza Palace was really Tony's fault, she hated scenes of any kind. In her home, even the most serious arguments were settled without anyone so much as raising his voice. Tony's eagerness to blunder into a confrontation had been embarrassing and a little bit scary.

Still, she resented being told what to do. Tara's interference had been bad enough. But now Olivia was insulting her by suggesting that she was a disgrace to the squad. "You're a fine one to lecture to me about letting down Coach Engborg," she told Olivia. "I wasn't the one who was late for practice the day the coach got hurt. And I'm not the one who's making trouble because I'm jealous of Mary Ellen."

"I am not jealous of Mary Ellen!" Olivia protested. "That's ridiculous!"

"Is it? I don't think so."

"If you're just going to change the subject by making crazy accusations, then there's no point in our talking," Olivia said before she walked out.

Hope returned to her practicing, but her mind was on Tony Pell. She was fairly sure that Tony would never get up his courage to call her. And normally she was too shy and reserved to ever consider calling a boy. But Muttsy gave her a ready-made excuse.

As soon as her last afternoon class ended, Hope went to the pay phone in the school lobby and phoned Tony's garage. Tony's vocational classes got out early, so he was already there working on a car when the call came through. "What's up?" he asked, obviously surprised to hear from Hope again. "Did someone claim the puppy?"

"No, it isn't that." Hope hesitated. "I was just

thinking that I'd like to visit Muttsy again. But I don't have any way of getting over there."

Tony's voice brightened. "No problem. I'll pick you up."

Ten minutes later, a chrome and red Harley-Davidson zoomed into the Tarenton High parking lot and came to a stop in front of the school's main entrance. There were still quite a few students milling around to witness the arrival of the notorious Tony Pell and to watch in amazement as quiet, petite Hope Chang emerged from the lobby and hopped onto the back of the enormous cycle with a practiced air.

Holly Hudson was standing with a group of Pompon Squad officers as Tony and Hope drove off, and she could hardly conceal her satisfaction. "See?" she crowed. "I told you that Hope was dating that hood."

Carla Simpson reddened. "I guess you're right."

Olivia was also watching Hope's departure from a few feet away, and she was indignant. Obviously, Hope had arranged this just to show what she thought of her advice. It was a direct snub to her leadership.

Actually, Hope hadn't really expected Tony to show up so quickly, while there were still so many students around to see. She almost had to force herself to leave the school lobby and take those few steps out to the waiting Harley. But in spite of her nervousness, she found that she was enjoying being the center of attention more than she would have thought possible. After this, her classmates wouldn't be so quick to dismiss her as a dull, timid grind. She'd show them!

Tony sensed Hope's mood and was happy to cooperate. "Shall we give them a show?" he whispered as Hope was strapping on the extra helmet.

"Good idea," she agreed.

"Hang on tight, then," he ordered.

The Harley lurched into gear and took off on a quick circuit of the parking lot, heading straight for the small hump in the pavement that was intended to force student cars to slow down as they entered from the road. Hope expected Tony to slow down or swerve around the obstacle at the last minute. Then she felt his muscles tense up under his heavy jacket, and she knew they were going over the bump. She clutched Tony's waist even tighter than before. Her heart felt as if it were bouncing up and down inside her chest.

The Harley took the bump at full speed. For a split second it was airborne. Then the wheels jounced back down on the pavement.

Hope swallowed hard. Amazingly, they were still upright and moving forward. She was aware of a few scattered whistles and cheers coming from the students who had witnessed the maneuver. For some crazy reason, she wanted to laugh.

At the first red light, Tony glanced back over his shoulder. "I hope I didn't scare you," he said.

"Not a bit," Hope lied. "It was exciting."

Tony's eyes widened. He'd been more than a little scared, himself.

"Good for you," he said, with more conviction

than he felt. "Then let's take a spin around the lake."

On the rest of the ride there were no more stunts, and Hope found that she was enjoying herself even more than she had the day before. Tony rode the Harley with the same complete concentration that Hope brought to studying, playing her violin, and cheerleading. Hope recognized Tony's skill, and it made her feel confident. Soon, she almost believed that she had never really been frightened.

After making a circuit of the winding road around the lake, they returned to the garage in town. Inside, there was the same purposeful clutter as the day before, and the same group of bored-looking cardplayers lounging around the table. Muttsy came waddling out of his corner and gave Tony a sloppy, affectionate greeting.

"He seems to have made himself at home here," Hope observed.

"I guess so," Tony said, obviously proud and delighted. "I take him home with me at night. My big brother likes him. But he seems happiest when he's here."

After they had made a fuss over the puppy, Tony noticed the sheet music sticking out of Hope's electric pink backpack. "I didn't know you played an instrument," he said. "Are you with a group or something?"

"Just the school orchestra. I play mostly classical violin."

"Oh. Right."

Hope felt a wave of confusion washing over her. She was starting to think Tony was more than just a muscle-bound guy with dreamy blue eyes. There was something wonderful about the way he seemed to show up just in time to ride off with her into the sunset. He was completely different from any of the boys at school.

Still, she couldn't imagine how they were ever going to get to know each other better if they didn't find something to talk about. Obviously, classical music was not going to be the subject that broke the ice.

Hope had always heard that the way to keep a conversation going was to show an interest in the other person and then be a good listener. Gamely, she tried to put the advice into practice. "What kind of music do you like?" she asked.

Tony shrugged. "I dunno. Anything that's on the radio. I don't think about it much."

"Oh." She thought a bit, then tried again. "It must be nice having an older brother. I've always wished I had one."

"It's okay," Tony mumbled.

"Tell me about your family," Hope encouraged him. "What does your brother do? Is he in college?"

"Hardly," Tony snickered. "Actually, right now he's on probation."

Hope was speechless.

"That's okay," Tony reassured her. "It isn't anything serious."

It was the strangest conversation in which Hope had ever been involved. She had never known anyone who had a family member on probation. How could it not be serious?

"Tell you what," suggested Tony after an awkward silence. "How would you like to see the car I've been working on?"

He led her to an ordinary-looking car in the back of the garage and proudly lifted the hood. Soon he had launched into an incomprehensible technical explanation about supercharging and extra carburetors. Hope hardly understood a word, but once again she was impressed by the way Tony exuded calm confidence when he talked about things he understood.

"This car may not look like much, but it'll do a hundred and twenty easy," he said, as he finished up his lecture. The way he said it, Hope knew he wasn't boasting. It was just a statement of fact.

"But what's the point?" she asked, mystified. "You can never drive it that fast. The speed limit is only fifty-five."

Tony grinned. "You really are a straight arrow."

"I am not," Hope protested.

"It's for racing," Tony explained. "There's a group of guys and girls who meet at midnight on Saturdays for road races. Mostly they use that two-mile loop of highway by Narrow Brook Lake. It's supposed to be closed at that time of night, but the state police never bother patroling there."

"Isn't it dangerous?"

"Not really. Not if you know what you're doing." Tony noticed the intrigued look in Hope's eyes and started to get worried. "It wouldn't be a place for you, though."

"Why not?" shot back Hope. "Do you think I'd be too scared?"

"Of course not." Tony squirmed. "It's just that you're too . . . too nice, I guess."

At the moment, the phrase sounded almost like an insult. Hope didn't mind being just plain nice. But who wanted to be "too nice"? Especially if it meant that Tony Pell wouldn't be interested in seeing her anymore.

After they finished admiring Tony's handiwork on the car, they rode to Dopey's, a local hangout that was famous for its barbecue sandwiches. This time, they managed to share a snack without running into anyone they knew from school. Then Tony took her home.

"Do you want to come in?" Hope asked, as they pulled up in front of the house.

Tony took one look at the Changs' modern ranch-style home and felt his knees go weak. Everything about the house was picture-perfect, from the perfectly manicured evergreen trees on the lawn to the stylish, narrow-slatted venetian blinds in the windows.

He could imagine the way Hope's mother would look him over if he dared to go inside. She'd be polite, of course, but her questions would probably be designed to make him feel about as welcome as a cockroach. For that matter, Tony wouldn't even blame her. He had no business dating Hope Chang. The whole world seemed to understand that — except for Hope, herself.

But Hope was a very smart girl, Tony told himself. Even though they didn't seem to have much in common, Hope must know better.

"Don't tell me you're afraid to come inside and meet my mom!" Hope chided him. "She can't hurt you. She'd even smaller than I am."

"You bet I'm afraid!"

Suddenly, Hope understood something. "It's the same way with my friends, isn't it?" she guessed aloud. "It isn't so much that you don't like them. You're just scared they won't like you.

"I'll make a deal with you," Hope said quickly. "If I go to the road race with you Saturday night, then you'll be nice to my friends on the squad. How about it?"

Tony swallowed hard. The truth was, he hadn't attended one of the midnight races in months. Ever since he almost got into big trouble over the car that turned out to be stolen, he had been doing his best to avoid anything that could bring him into contact with the police. But Hope's offer sounded like a challenge to him, and he couldn't let himself back down from a challenge. "Okay," he agreed. "It's a deal."

"Good."

Impulsively, Hope planted a kiss on Tony's cheek. He was so startled that after she disappeared into the house he almost flooded the Harley's engine trying to get it started.

CHAPTER

As soon as Hope let herself into the house, her mother appeared in the door to the spacious room at the back of the house that she used as a studio. Mrs. Chang was a small, slender woman who wore a size-six dress and spent much of her time painting watercolors of flowers. But she could be very strict when she thought the situation called for it, and Hope did not look forward to being on the receiving end of one of her mother's lectures.

"Did I hear a motorcycle in the driveway?" Mrs. Chang asked.

"Yes, I suppose so," said Hope, thinking what a dumb answer *that* was. There was no *supposing* about it.

A dreamy look came into Mrs. Chang's eyes. "Isn't that nice," she said.

"It is?" Hope was so startled she almost choked.

"When I was in graduate school I used to date a young man who owned a cycle," Mrs. Chang reminisced. "I don't think I ever had so much fun!"

Hope's eyes opened wide. She had certainly never heard that story before. She was waiting for more details, but her mother abruptly changed the subject. "I do wish, however, that you would invite your young man in," she said. "If you're going to be riding on a motorcycle, I would like to know who is in control. Those machines can be dangerous."

"Oh, he's very safety conscious," Hope insisted. "I always wear a helmet. But I think he's a little shy about coming in to meet you."

All this was true. But Hope was still taken aback when her mother seemed ready to accept it at face value. "I understand how that can be," she said sympathetically. "Shyness can be so difficult to overcome."

Mrs. Chang went back to work, and Hope poured herself a glass of orange juice and took it to her room. Her mother could be so trusting. She hated to think how hurt both her parents would be if she were ever caught with Tony at an illegal road race!

The obvious way to avoid hurting her folks was to call off her challenge to Tony and stay away from him from now on. But if she did that she would be no better than all the other kids who put down Tony without knowing the truth about him. For that matter, she'd be worse than the others because she had already gone out of her way to convince him that she was his friend.

Besides, why should she let gossips like Diana Tucker and Holly Hudson run her life? Everyone knew that Diana and Holly were troublemakers. Normally, Olivia wouldn't have taken their advice on anything. But where she, Hope, was concerned, there seemed to be a different standard at work. Even Olivia, who was supposed to be one of her friends, thought she was too naive to be trusted.

She couldn't get her mind off Tony all that evening, and when she got to school on Friday, she was still half in a daze. Sitting in her American history class, she realized that she had no idea at all what the teacher, Ms. Conway, was talking about. The chapter they were discussing had been assigned a week ago, but she had been so preoccupied that she hadn't got around to reading it yet. Fortunately, she volunteered comments so often that Ms. Conway hardly ever called on her.

It was just Hope's bad luck, though, that Ms. Conway had picked that day to do things differently.

"Hope," she said brightly at the beginning of the discussion period, "why don't you start things off by explaining what the Missouri Compromise was?"

"The what?" Hope felt as if she'd just been mugged. The question took her completely by surprise. Usually with Ms. Conway, if you didn't know the answer to the question you could just change the subject by asking *her* a question about something else. But at the moment, Hope's mind was a complete blank.

"The Missouri Compromise," Ms. Conway repeated. "Can you tell us what it is?"

"Well," began Hope, desperately waiting for inspiration to strike, "it had to do with Missouri. And, well, they decided to compromise."

Someone in the back of the room giggled. Ms. Conway looked as if she had just sucked on a lemon. "Not even a good try, Hope," she said. "I thought I could count on you to at least make an effort to do the reading. You've let me down. Perhaps you've been devoting too much time to your extracurricular activities."

The giggler in the back of the room started up all over again, and this time she was not alone. Of course, Ms. Conway had been thinking of cheerleading and orchestra practice, but that wasn't what the others were thinking of. Someone — Hope was sure it was Bill Hadley — hummed the opening bars of "Leader of the Pack" and Diana Tucker let out a little squeal of appreciation.

"That's quite enough from the music section," Ms. Conway snapped.

Fortunately, Jerry Johnson, over in the first row, could be counted on to be oblivious to the joke. He already had his hand up, and Ms. Conway turned her attention to him. Hope wished she could crawl under her chair. She was sure she wasn't the only one in class who didn't know what the Missouri Compromise was. There were plenty of students who flubbed answers all the time. So why was it that when she messed up just one time, Ms. Conway acted as if it were some sort of personal betrayal?

By the time the class bell rang, Hope was no longer embarrassed. She was steaming mad. On her way out of the room she practically bowled over Holly Hudson, who was standing with Diana just outside the classroom door. The smirk on Holly's face told Hope at once who was responsible for starting the mass giggling attack.

"That was you, wasn't it?" Hope blurted out.

"I couldn't help it," Holly said amiably. "I just never thought I'd hear Hope Chang say anything so dumb."

"That's right," chimed in Diana. "Even I could have done a better job of faking it."

"I don't doubt it," Hope shot back. "You've had a lot more practice being a fake than I have."

"At least I don't hang out with criminals," Diana sniffed.

"Tony is not a criminal! You take that back!"

Diana made a pouty face. "Don't be silly. Your boyfriend couldn't get away with threatening me, and you can't, either."

"I'm not threatening you!" Hope all but shouted. By now she was starting to feel a little bit silly. There was no way she could win this argument, so the best thing would be to make a dignified retreat.

Hope hitched her backpack up onto her shoulder and started to edge past Diana. Unfortunately, Holly picked that moment to intervene. "Come on, let's not fight," she said, latching on to Hope's elbow.

As Hope turned to answer Holly, her pack bumped against Diana's arm. "Hey! You shoved me!" Diana exclaimed, giving Hope's arm a quick but hard shove in return.

"Stop that!" protested Hope, more shocked than hurt.

Holly was always quick to get excited. "Don't fight!" she all but screeched as she grabbed Hope again and tried to pull her toward the other side of the hall.

Hope instinctively tried to pull away, but Holly had a tight grip on her elbow. They were in midtussle when Ms. Conway's broad form suddenly appeared in the doorway. "What's going on here?" she demanded.

"Hope started it!" Diana volunteered. "She pushed me!"

"This is outrageous," Ms. Conway huffed. "I won't have cat fights breaking out in front of my classroom. And as for you," she added, shaking her finger at Hope, "I am truly appalled. Appalled!"

"But Ms. Conway, it isn't what you think . . ." Hope sputtered.

Ms. Conway regarded her, hands on hips. "I don't want to hear any excuses. You girls can report to Mrs. Oetjen's office and settle your differences there."

Hope felt as if she must be having a nightmare. She had never been sent to the principal's office before. Not once in twelve years of school. This couldn't be happening!

Holly was almost as upset as Hope. But Diana, a veteran of many interviews with many school principals, was cool and collected. While they waited in the outer office, she pulled out a nail file and made minor repairs on her talon-length purple nails.

A few minutes later, Mrs. Oetjen called them in. Peering over the tops of her bifocals, she studied the three girls with a frown. "All right. Who wants to go first?"

"It was all my fault," Holly blurted out. "See, it started with the Missouri Compromise. I didn't mean to giggle. I just couldn't help it. Bill was behind me in class, because he likes to sit in the back row. And he was singing that line from 'Leader of the Pack.' The one with the motorcycle sounds. You know, 'Vroom, vrooom.' Then I just wanted to make peace. That's when Hope shoved Diana — "

"I did not," Hope interrupted.

Mrs. Oetjen motioned for Hope to be quiet. "Let Holly talk," she said. "Although, I must say, so far I don't understand a word. Do you mean to say you were fighting over the Missouri Compromise?"

"No, see, the way it was. . . ." Holly was prepared to launch into another lengthy explanation, but this time Diana took over.

"It was just a little misunderstanding, Mrs. Oetjen," she said. "We're all sorry. It won't happen again."

"That's more like it." The principal looked relieved. "I want each of you to do twenty minutes of detention in homeroom after school today. And in the future, try to adopt the spirit of compromise in settling your own arguments."

Half a minute later they were dismissed. "Whew," sighed Holly, as she led the way out into the hall. "Thanks for cutting in, Diana. I was just talking us all into deeper trouble."

"You've got a lot to learn about handling authority types," Diana said, studying her reflection in the glass front of the school trophy case. "When people like Mrs. Oetjen ask what happened, they don't really want to know what happened. They're just hoping you'll apologize, and then they won't have to waste their time."

"But that's so unjust!" Hope protested. "Besides, I don't believe that of Mrs. Oetjen. You're too cynical, Diana."

Holly stared at her. "I don't see what you're complaining about, Hope. Twenty minutes of detention is nothing. If it weren't for Diana, we'd probably be in a lot worse trouble than that."

If it weren't for Diana, we wouldn't be in trouble at all, Hope thought. Besides, it wasn't the twenty minutes that bothered her. It was the principle involved. Didn't anyone care that she was innocent? Apparently not.

No wonder Tony thinks I'm naive, she lectured herself. If this can happen to me, imagine what Tarenton High must have been like for him. Maybe I have been too cautious all my life. If you're going to get in trouble, anyway, why not have a little fun along the way?

While Hope's mind simmered with thoughts of rebellion, Sean Dubrow was learning that domesticity was harder than he had ever dreamed possible. Six-thirty Friday evening found him standing in his kitchen, up to his wrists in a gooey mixture of hamburger meat, chopped onion, and bread crumbs.

"I can't believe this is ever going to turn out to be edible," he wailed.

"It's probably okay," Kate said not very confidently, as she wiped away a tear that was making its way down Sean's cheek. "Anyway, it isn't worth crying about."

"I'm not crying. The onions are making my eyes water."

If Sean were the type who cried easily, no doubt he would have been shedding real tears by now. The cooking was hardly begun, and already the Dubrow kitchen looked like a disaster scene. In his search for the meatloaf pan, Sean had been forced to rummage through every cabinet in the room, and in the process he had droppd a canister of flour. His efforts to sweep the stuff up had only succeeded in leaving a whitish film on the tile floor. In the meantime, every surface in the kitchen was stacked with grocery bags, pans, and miscellaneous debris.

So far, the only actual cooking he had done was to prepare a tray of cheese puff appetizers, Windy's specialty. The pastry puffs were already in the freezer — Windy always had them on hand, ready to pop into the oven on short notice. But instead of making a homemade cheese sauce to fill them with, as Windy did, Sean had decided to play it safe by using one of those ready-to-eat cheese spreads that came in an aerosol can. The idea had sounded simple enough, but the results were not very appetizing. When he removed the tray from the oven, the puffs themselves were still half-frozen and the cheese filling had melted into puddles of orange goop.

In the meantime, his father was upstairs taking a shower, still unaware that Marge Kopecky was about to arrive at any minute. Sean had explained to his dad that he and Kate were fixing him a birthday dinner, but even before he could mention that a guest was invited, there had been a squabble.

Alarmed by the smell of burning cheese spread that had dripped off the side of the baking pan and onto the bottom of the oven, Mr. Dubrow had come into the kitchen and surveyed the mess.

"Don't you think you should wait until Kate gets here?" he asked his son.

"Not really. Kate doesn't know any more about cooking than I do," Sean explained. "Our deal was that I'd take care of the meal and she'd bring dessert."

Mr. Dubrow frowned. "Call me old-fashioned, but in my day cooking was the woman's job. Anyway, I would have thought that a girl like Kate would know her way around a kitchen."

"What do you mean 'a girl like Kate'?" Sean asked suspiciously.

"No offense," his father said. "But Kate isn't exactly the glamor-girl type. She doesn't bother to fix herself up to look cute. She contradicts every other word you say. Now she's got you in the kitchen. Seems to me that girl has you completely buffaloed."

"Kate didn't get me into the kitchen," Sean said

through clenched teeth. "This dinner was my idea."

But as his father retreated upstairs to the shower, Sean had to wonder if there wasn't some truth to his dad's complaint. Until he met Kate, he'd been perfectly content with his role as Mr. Macho of Tarenton High. True, he fell in love on the average of once a week, but being in love had never seriously cramped his style. Now here he was plotting to get his dad married off. And not even to please Kate herself — to please her family!

Sean had been just starting to feel really resentful when Kate arrived, carrying a large white cake box from Olson's bakery. "Just like my family always serves," she said cheerfully, pointing to the box. "Actually, I thought about trying to bake a cake myself, but tonight didn't seem the time to experiment."

After that, Sean's resentment began to melt away. Kate might not be his dad's idea of glamorous, but to him, she looked just fine. The casual slacks she liked to wear just emphasized her incredibly long, slender legs. And this evening, she was wearing a wheat-colored turtleneck sweater that complemented her pale, freckled complexion.

Best of all, Kate had a positive energy that lifted Sean's spirits. Unlike a lot of girls, who seemed to stand around as if they were challenging him to impress them, Kate had spunk. Within minutes of her arrival, she had set about straightening up some of the worst of the mess and setting the table.

Soon, the meatloaf was ready for the oven and Kate was examining the contents of a pot that was simmering on the stove.

"Mashed potatoes," he explained. "I had a quite a struggle getting them through the ricer. I don't know where Windy finds the muscle power to do the job."

Kate took another look inside the pot and wrinkled her nose. "I hate to be the one to break the news," she said, "but I think you're supposed to cook the potatoes before you put them through the ricer. Not after."

"Oh, no! You've got to be kidding!"

"Honest. I'm serious."

But no sooner were the words out, than Kate started laughing so hard that she collapsed onto a kitchen chair. "I'm sorry," she apologized between bursts of laughter. "I know it must not seem funny to you. But I just had a mental picture of Superman Sean doing battle with a sack of potatoes."

"I guess it was pretty funny," Sean admitted. "I kept thinking that Windy must be secretly working out with my weights."

They were still trying to compose themselves when Marge Kopecky rang the doorbell. Mrs. Kopecky had a plump figure and was certainly no more the glamorous type than Kate, but she never appeared in public without three-inch heels, red polish on her nails, and false eyelashes — just the accessories that his dad considered essential to feminine appeal.

Sean liked Marge in spite of her style, not because of it. He liked her so much, in fact, that he had let himself forget that Marge might not find it easy to fit in with the informal spirit of the evening.

Almost as soon as she took off her coat, Mrs. Kopecky began to look uneasy. "Where are the other guests?" she asked, peering around as if she expected them to pop out from behind the drapes or under the sofa.

"There aren't any," Sean said, turning on the charm. "This was a last-minute idea, so we planned an intimate dinner for four."

A few minutes later, Sean excused himself, leaving Kate to deal with the awkward moment when his father would come into the living room and discover Marge. There were times, he thought, when being the cook wasn't such a bad idea.

Returning to the kitchen, he decided to cut his losses. The pasty mass of cooked potatoes went into the garbage, along with the half-burned, half-frozen cheese puffs. He grabbed a box of fast-cooking rice from the corner cabinet and began to study the directions.

The meal he eventually put on the table wouldn't have won any prizes. The meatloaf was on the dry side. The rice was sticky, even though the instructions on the box promised "perfect results every time." The frozen vegetables were frozen vegetables. Still, no one ran screaming from the table when Sean served the food.

Kate kept the conversation going by talking about the sports clinic and then working the subject around to flying. Then Marge took over and told stories about some of the crazy types who had showed up at her charter service wanting to hire planes — like one guy who had a mysterious map that belonged to his grandfather and wanted a pilot to fly the pontoon plane to a remote lake, where he expected to find a lost gold mine.

"When the pilot picked him up again, the guy was disgusted," Marge laughed. "It turned out the x on the map was the location of a secret fishing hole, not a lost mine — Only this guy hadn't bothered to take his fishing gear with him."

After they'd blown out the candles on the birthday cake, Sean went out to the kitchen to fix some coffee. He was busy setting up the automatic coffeepot when Marge joined him.

"I appreciate all the effort you went to," she told him, "and the evening turned out pretty well. But do you mind if I give you some advice?"

"I can guess what it is," Sean said. "Give up trying to arrange my dad's social life, right?"

Marge smiled. "That's about it."

"I'm sorry if I put you on the spot."

"No problem." Marge chuckled. "I felt a lot more relaxed once I realized that this was your idea, not your father's. Your father is a really nice man. But between my job and trying to keep the charter service going, I'm too busy right now to get serious about anyone. I thought he and I had just worked that out, so I was a little bit surprised to be invited to a family dinner."

Marge carried the coffee cups into the dining room, leaving Sean to figure out the implications of her remark.

"What do you suppose she meant when she said she and my dad had 'worked that out'?" Sean asked Kate later in the evening, when they were stacking the dishwasher together. "Does that mean that Dad already asked Marge to marry him and she turned him down?"

Kate shrugged. "I don't know. Why don't you ask him?"

"I can't do that," Sean said quickly. "What if Marge wasn't the first? What if Dad has been looking for a wife all along? What if he's proposed to other women before and been turned down? I can't ask him about that kind of thing. It's too personal."

Kate finished stacking the dessert plates just in time to catch her glasses as they were about to slide off the tip of her nose. "I can't figure you out," she observed. "You can walk into a room full of complete strangers and wow them with your dazzling personality. How come you can't talk about personal subjects with your own father?"

"I don't know. That's just the way it is."

Gently, he took out of her hands the stack of dirty dishes she was holding and pulled her close. "I don't mind getting personal with you, though," he said.

"That's good," Kate sighed as she planted a tender, searching kiss on Sean's lips.

Even if he was a lousy cook and a disaster at matchmaking, kissing was one skill that Sean knew he was good at. But as he returned Kate's kiss, he couldn't help wondering if he was measuring up to her expectations. Kate was different from any girl he had ever dated. Good looks and a flashy car weren't enough for her. She wanted a guy who knew how to communicate, who could put his deepest feelings into words.

Sean wasn't even sure that he had any deep feelings.

As he held Kate close, he heard a little voice inside his head warning him to be careful. He and his dad had been getting along great just being buddies until Kate had influenced him to try to change the rules. Now she seemed to want him to deal with a lot of personal subjects that he'd just as soon ignore.

Where was it all going to end?

Someday, Sean thought, Kate is going to wake up and realize that I'm basically a very average, shallow kind of guy. All I can do is keep her fooled for as long as possible. But how long can that be?

CHAPTER

When Mary Ellen Tilford pulled into the Tarenton High parking lot on Saturday evening, the first thing she noticed was a huge banner hung over the school's main doors, bearing the hand-painted words: CRUSH THE COUGARS.

The slogan wasn't exactly sweet and senti-mental, but Mary Ellen had to fight hard to hold back tears of nostalgia. School spirit had always meant a lot to her. Just a year ago, she had been Tarenton High's number one spirit leader, the girl who could cheer harder and with more en-thusiasm than anyone else. Now her role was different. She was an assistant coach, and she was expected to be cool, organized, and above all, adult at all times.

She wondered if any of her old schoolmates realized just how terrified she was.

So far, nothing had gone right. Olivia, her old

friend from last year, was barely speaking to her. Of the other cheerleaders, Mary Ellen thought Hope Chang and Sean Dubrow were the most solid, but Hope had been in a daze all week, and Sean didn't seem quite sure how to act with a coach who was close to his own age.

Peter Rayman and Tara Armstrong had been friendly, but Mary Ellen was a little bit wary of both of them. Peter was a lot like Walt Manners had been last year. He loved to dance and choreograph so much that if she wasn't careful, he'd turn the whole squad into his personal dance troupe. On the other hand, behind his outgoing exterior there was a core of sensitivity. Hurt his feelings, and it might be a long time before he would give you a second chance.

As for Tara, she was beautiful and high-spirited. Still, Mary Ellen suspected her of being a little light in the common sense department.

The only member of the squad Mary Ellen felt really comfortable with was Jessica Bennett. Now that she and Pres were married, Jessica had finally gotten over seeing her as a rival for Patrick Henley's love. During the last few weeks, they had become friends.

Mary Ellen parked the car and carried her bag into the coach's office. She felt a little odd about changing in the cubicle in the office and locking her bag in the drawer of the coach's desk. If only Coach Engborg hadn't twisted her knee!

Thank goodness the coach would be back soon. All she had to do was to get through this one game without making any serious mistakes.

Much to her relief, Jessica was the first squad member to come out of the girls' locker room. "Hi, there," Mary Ellen said. "Did Patrick call you? Pres is helping him out today. He and Pres are coming to the game directly from work. Then later, I thought we could go out for hamburgers."

"Uh-huh," said Jessica without enthusiasm. She had her own idea of what she and Patrick would be doing after the game. There was a postgame dance at the social hall of the church that she wanted to go to. But it was for high school students and their dates only. Mary Ellen and Pres couldn't get in even if they wanted to, which they probably wouldn't. There was no sense upsetting Mary Ellen before the game by bringing up the subject, Jessica told herself. She'd deal with that later.

One by one, the other cheerleaders appeared and started to do their pregame warm-ups. The cheerleaders for the Washington Cougars arrived and stopped to chat for a few minutes before taking up their station near the visiting team bench.

"Before we get started, I want to have a brief meeting," Mary Ellen told the squad. She explained that the head of the after-school sports clinic had been in touch with Coach Engborg to ask about the cheerleaders putting on a demonstration for their open house the next afternoon. The coach thought it was a wonderful idea, since she was always in favor of the squad doing community service work. But since the open house was on a Sunday, and they'd been invited on short

101

notice, Coach Engborg was making participation optional.

"How many of you think you'll be able to take part?" Mary Ellen finished up.

Naturally, Sean was the first to say yes, since the plan had been Kate's idea.

Olivia agreed, too. She was miffed that all this had been arranged without anyone consulting her first. After all, she was the captain! But then it was probably her fault for not going to visit the coach since the accident. She had been planning to go this week, but she kept putting it off.

Peter and Tara were also quick to say they'd be at the clinic. Both of them were always happy to have an opportunity to strut their stuff in front of an audience, even one made up mostly of grade school kids.

After a moment's thought, Jessica agreed, too. "If Patrick was going to be free tomorrow, I'd be tempted to say no," she admitted. "But he has a big job. He'll be busy all afternoon."

"On Sunday?" Peter asked. "H & T's TLC Moving must be getting awfully busy."

"It's a very special job, too," Jessica told him, her voice filled with pride. "That big auction barn over at Hart's Corners is having an estate sale. There are quite a few valuable antiques in the sale, good silver and so on, and they got nervous about storing the stuff in the barn all week. So they transferred all of it to H & T's warehouse. Of course, Patrick has to move the stuff back tomorrow before the auction. Pres is going to help, too — right, Mary Ellen? It's a big secret."

"It *was* a big secret. Until now." Mary Ellen said pointedly.

Jessica flashed a grin that showed off her dimples. "Don't be silly. What difference can it make if the squad knows? They aren't going to tell anyone."

Mary Ellen decided to drop the subject. She didn't want to give the impression that she distrusted any of her cheerleaders. It was just that she and Jessica obviously didn't have the same definition of a secret.

Suddenly, it occurred to her that one member of the squad hadn't said whether or not she'd be at the open house. "What about you, Hope?" she asked.

"Huh?" Hope looked as if her mind were a million miles away.

"Earth calling Hope," Peter joked.

Hope still looked blank.

"The open house," Mary Ellen prompted. "Tomorrow afternoon. At the sports clinic."

"Okay," said Hope. "Why not?"

"I'll put that down as a yes," said Mary Ellen. "Unenthusiastic as it may be."

Hope didn't seem to recognize that she was being gently scolded. Outwardly, she was the same Hope Chang as ever. Her straight black hair was shining clean and carefully combed. Her uniform and shoes were immaculate. Her moves, as Mary Ellen led the squad through a last-minute warm-up, were correct in every way.

Still, everyone could see that Hope was not herself, and they knew her worries must have something to do with Tony Pell.

As he put his arms around Hope's waist to partner her in a practice lift, Pete felt how taut her muscles were. Hope was so stiff tonight that she seemed almost ready to shatter, like a delicate porcelain doll.

One part of Peter wanted to know as little about Hope's relationship with Tony as possible. It didn't matter that he and Hope hadn't dated in weeks. Jealousy wasn't always a rational emotion.

But he had promised himself that he would stay friends with Hope, no matter how hard it might be sometimes.

As the warm-up drew to a close, he took Hope aside. "I want you to know," he said, "that I'm always here if you need someone to talk to. I can see that you haven't been yourself ever since you started seeing Tony. If he's giving you a hard time — "

Hope cut him off before he could finish his sentence. "Tony isn't giving me a hard time," she said bitterly. "It's my so-called friends who are giving me a hard time. If everyone trusts me so much, how come no one trusts my judgment about Tony?"

Before Peter could think of an answer, Hope stalked off to join the others.

The squad was lining up for the opening locomotive, and as Peter took his place, Hope deliberately walked around to the other end of the line to stand next to Sean. *Ouch*, thought Peter, that really hurt! Even when they were having problems, Hope hadn't let their personal differences stand in the way of their cheering together.

Olivia noticed Hope's last-minute move, but it was too late now to handle the problem without making a scene. The crowd was in the stands. All eyes were on the squad. And the opening whistle of the game was just moments away. As unobtrusively as possible, Olivia tapped Jessica on the shoulder and motioned for her to take Hope's usual position. Then she picked up the megaphone.

"Okay, Wolves fans!" Olivia shouted. "Are you ready to cheer?"

"YES!!" came the answer.

"Good! Then let's hear it, loud and clear! Do I hear a *W?*"

"W!" the fans roared.

Sean, flanked by Tara and Hope, formed a human *W.* Then, as Olivia called out the letter *O,* Hope and Tara joined hands in an arc, and Sean barreled between them in a quick series of forward rolls, ending with a handstand and a spring to a standing position.

From there, the routine continued letter by letter. It wasn't quite as effective as usual, since Hope was shorter than Jessica. But Olivia felt sure that no one in the stands noticed.

In a way, though, it was lucky that Coach Engborg had missed this particular game. If Hope had refused to do her usual part when the coach was around, there would have been real fireworks, Olivia thought glumly.

For the rest of the evening, the squad had its work cut out for it.

The game against Washington was supposed to be one of the least important on Tarenton High's schedule. The Cougars were not a good team; they hadn't beaten the Wolves in over five years. To make matters worse, the game had been re-scheduled because the gym was needed for a regional teachers' conference on Friday evening. The crowd was the smallest Olivia had seen all season long, and although they cheered enthusiastically in the beginning, it was hard to expect such a small group to keep shouting through four whole quarters of play.

"This feels more like a practice than a real game," Olivia whispered to Tara a few minutes into the first period.

"It sure does," Tara agreed. "I just wish the Cougars realized that."

Tara was right. Seeing a chance to engineer an upset, the Cougars were taking advantage of the Wolves' relaxed mood to build up an early lead.

By the end of the first period, the Cougars were five points ahead, and still the Wolves' starting five acted unworried, confident they could forge ahead at any time.

By the half, the Cougars had widened their advantage to nine points.

During the third quarter, the Wolves seemed to wake up. They played hard, but their timing was not quite right. Shots that should have been easy were bouncing off the rim of the basket, off the backboard — everywhere but through the hoop.

The beginning of the fourth quarter was more

of the same. Some Tarenton rooters were leaving in disgust. Even the Pompon Squad seemed stunned into immobility.

When the Wolves' coach called a time out, Olivia decided to take the opportunity to hold a conference with the squad. There had to be something they could do to wake up the Wolves' cheering section — or what was left of it. A dramatic move was called for.

"Can't we at least do a pyramid?" Olivia begged Mary Ellen.

"Sorry." Mary Ellen was firm. She had her orders.

The next best thing was the "We're the Wolves" fight song, a number that included some flashy cartwheels and leaps. Olivia was about to call for it when she noticed that Hope was nowhere around.

"Where is that girl?" she groused.

Peter Rayman pointed silently toward the door at the back of the gym. Tony Pell was standing just inside the swinging door, his motorcycle helmet dangling from one arm. Hope was beside him, deep in a whispered conversation.

"This is the last straw," Olivia fumed. "I'm going to talk this out with Hope right now."

Olivia stormed off to deal with Hope, while the others stood there, momentarily dumbstruck.

Behind them, the crowd exploded with excitement.

On the court, Bill Hadley had stolen the ball in midpass and made a fantastic shot, almost from midcourt. The ball sailed through the hoop cleanly, and the crowd roared again. Suddenly, the Wolves had come alive.

Everyone was wild with joy — except the Tarenton High cheerleaders. From her place on the sidelines, Mary Ellen ached with frustration. Olivia and Hope were nowhere around, and the rest of the squad was woolgathering, their attention focused on something that was going on at the back of the gym.

Jessica was the first of the cheerleaders to react to Bill's fantastic shot. Realizing that someone had better take over, she sprinted toward Olivia's abandoned megaphone.

She was just about to pick it up, when Mary Ellen beat her to it. Carried away by the emotion of the moment, Mary Ellen forgot she was a coach.

"We're in the groove," she shouted. "We're on the move. . . ."

It was just like old times.

Or almost. The last echoes of the cheer had hardly faded when Jessica snatched the megaphone from Mary Ellen's hand. "Why do you have to be so greedy?" she hissed. "You had your year to be the sweetheart of Tarenton High. You had Patrick wrapped around your little finger, and you didn't even want him. Now you have Pres. Why can't you stand back and give the rest of us a chance?"

Mary Ellen felt as if she'd been slapped. She knew it was wrong of her to get carried away like that, but it had only been for a minute. The fans in the bleachers seemed to have hardly noticed.

And to hear those words from Jessica, of all people!

Fighting back the tears, Mary Ellen retreated to her seat. For the rest of the game, her face was a mask of hurt and disappointment.

On the court, the Wolves' luck had changed dramatically. Tarenton High finished the game in a blaze of glory, scoring twelve straight points and winning the game, 68–63.

Olivia and Hope returned in time to help lead the cheers in the tumultuous final minutes. But the revived squad spirit did not last past the final whistle.

As soon as she had shaken the hands of the visiting cheerleaders, Hope stalked out of the auditorium, not even bothering to change into her street clothes.

Jessica at least took the time to shower and change, but her mood was grim. "I see now why you didn't want Mary Ellen as assistant coach," she told Olivia through clenched teeth. "This is an impossible situation."

There was no question now of going out with Pres and Mary Ellen for hamburgers. Patrick and Jessica drove in silence to the dance at the church hall.

Patrick said nothing until they were on the dance floor together, moving to the beat of a slow ballad.

"You're my girl, Jessica," he said. "You know I'm on your side, no matter what. But aren't you being a little bit hard on Mary Ellen?"

"I am not!" Jessica protested. But it was hard to stay angry, with Patrick's arms enfolding her. Patrick could be impetuous, even selfish at times, but in all the time she had known him, he had never once said a mean word about anyone.

"I'm ashamed to admit it," she confessed, "but in a way, I'm still jealous of Mary Ellen."

Patrick held her closer. "That's ridiculous! You know there's nothing between me and Mary Ellen. She's married!"

Jessica shook her head. "It isn't that. I'm not jealous of you. I guess I'm jealous because she was such a perfect cheerleader. And now she's still around, reminding us at every practice of just how perfect she was."

Patrick laughed. "That doesn't sound like the Mary Ellen I knew. Believe me, she's had her problems, too."

"Maybe you're right," Jessica said slowly.

"I know I am," Patrick told her. "You're jealous of a myth, Jessica. I think the time has come for you to stop concentrating on Mary Ellen, and follow your own star."

Jessica looked up at Patrick, her green eyes swimming with tears of relief and happiness. Patrick was right, of course. She had worked herself up over nothing.

But what did that mean, exactly, "Follow your own star"?

Later that evening, after she'd kissed Patrick good-night, she would spend a long time in her darkened bedroom, staring out the window. It was a clear North Country night, and the sky seemed almost ablaze with stars. How could she possibly pick out her personal star from all the others?

And would her star lead her to a lifetime with Patrick?

To college?

Or to a completely different future that she couldn't even begin to imagine?

CHAPTER

Tony Pell was nervous.

"I don't think this is such a good idea," he said.

"What's the matter?" Hope challenged him. "Don't tell me you're afraid."

"Who said anything about being afraid?"

"Then let's go."

Gritting his teeth, Tony turned the key in the ignition of the white Mustang. The car had a little something extra under the hood, and the sound of its engine turning over filled the garage with a satisfyingly loud roar. Tony pulled out onto the street, then got out to shut the garage door behind him.

When he returned to the driver's seat, he glanced over at Hope to see if she had changed her mind.

The determined look on her face told him there was no point in arguing anymore. Hope looks so delicate and fragile, but when she sets her mind on something, Tony thought with amazement, she's a lot tougher than I am!

Tony wasn't sure why, but the mere accusation that he might be afraid to race tonight was enough to make him determined to prove himself.

His problem was with the crowd that gathered to take part in the midnight road races. Some of them were nice enough people who just loved fast driving and didn't have any place that was strictly legal where they could practice their skills. Other regular members of the group weren't so nice at all. He knew that just being around those guys was a sure way to get into trouble.

"They're just not the kind of people a nice girl like you should hang around with," he'd told Hope when he stopped in at the basketball game to try to get her to change her mind.

But Hope wouldn't take his word for it. "First you told me how much fun it was to race," she reminded him. "You said it wasn't dangerous at all. Then as soon as I got interested, you changed your tune."

Tony didn't have the courage to admit that he'd just been bragging, trying to impress the cute little cheerleader who seemed so naive about his world. Now he was stuck with his own lies.

What he really wanted to do with Hope was to take her out on a nice, normal date. They could go to a movie. Or out to Benny's for a hamburger and fries.

But, of course, if Hope wanted to do those things, she had a choice of dozens of guys who would be happy to take her out. Guys who could fit in with her clean-cut friends. Guys who wouldn't feel terrified at the very thought of stepping inside her super-neat, modern house to meet her parents.

As he drove toward the entrance to the highway, Tony gripped the wheel with his fingers crossed on both hands. It was awful how you could consider all the alternatives and still end up doing something that you knew was stupid.

The entrance to the road was officially closed. A thick metal chain with a big KEEP OUT sign hanging from it was strung between the stone gatehouses that guarded the entrance.

As if he did this sort of thing every day, Tony got out to move the chain, then motioned for Hope to drive the Mustang through the gate.

It was at that moment that Hope felt her courage starting to desert her. She had been thinking that attending the races was a big lark, a way of proving to herself that Hope Chang wasn't just a robot who was programmed to study, practice the violin, and cheer. Now it was beginning to hit home that she was doing more than breaking a few silly rules. She was breaking the law!

"Don't worry," Tony rationalized as he got back in the car after replacing the chain. "If they really didn't want us in here, they'd use a padlock, right?"

They drove to the top of the hill and pulled into a small lot adjacent to a scenic overlook. There were already about dozen cars parked there, and about twice that many people were standing around in small groups, talking.

Hope had expected the cars to be flashy, but

most of them were quite ordinary. All of them were at least a few years old, and more than a few looked as if they'd been involved in recent fender-benders.

"I know they don't look like much," said Tony, reading her mind. "But these babies have got speed. There's no sense in advertising that to the smokies, though."

"I guess not," said Hope doubtfully.

She had all but forgotten that she was still wearing her cheerleading uniform, but almost as soon as she got out of the Mustang, a few of the guys spotted her red and white pleated skirt. "Whadda ya' know?" one of them called out. "Tony's brought his own cheerleader along. Little Miss High School!"

A tall girl with black hair and a cigarette drooping out of her mouth yelled back at the heckler. "Hey! shut up an' be nice," she commanded him. "She's Tony's friend."

"Hi there, Marla." Tony greeted the girl like an old friend, and introduced her to Hope. "Why don't you two talk for a few seconds?" he suggested. "I've got to check out tonight's ground rules."

Marla made small talk for a few minutes, explaining to Hope how the race would be run in two-car heats. She was clearly trying to make Hope feel at ease, but when it became obvious that Hope knew nothing about cars, the conversation ground to a dead halt. Soon, Marla spotted someone she wanted to talk to on the other side of the pull-off. Hope retreated to a wooden bench back in the shadows near the overlook guard rail.

The bench was dry, and she felt less conspicuous sitting down.

She had just gotten comfortable when two guys in their twenties came out of the men's restroom and stopped to talk near the bank of outdoor phones.

"It's all set," the larger of the men said to the shorter one. "I've got a fence lined up for the silver."

"Okay, okay," mumbled the short one. "But I still don't like the set-up. What about the driver?"

"Don't worry about him. It ain't his stuff, Right? We just grab the truck, all nice and packed full of antiques for us, and take off. Simple."

Hope felt the goose bumps on her arms, even under her warm sweater and down jacket. The meaning of the conversation didn't quite sink in, but she had seen enough crime shows on television to know what a fence was. She knew it would not be good at all if the men noticed her presence, and she was relieved when they wandered away without so much as a glance in her direction.

Even then, she was too scared to move.

She sat there, shivering, until Tony found her.

"Hey, Hope!" he said, when he spotted her. "I've been looking all over for you. My heat is starting any minute now."

Hope followed him over to the Mustang and slipped into the passenger seat before he could protest. "I want to ride with you," she announced.

"Come on, Hope. I don't think that's such a hot idea."

Hope sneaked a glance at the knot of spectators standing around Marla. The two men she had just overheard were there on the fringe of the group. It was probably just her imagination, but she couldn't help thinking that one of them was staring at her in a funny way. She was scared to ride with Tony, and more scared still not to.

When Tony realized that nothing would budge her, he shrugged in defeat and started the engine. Very slowly, they pulled up to the starting line.

"Are you sure you want to do this?" Tony asked her.

"Of course I'm sure. But what happens if the police come?" she asked.

"They won't come. They never do."

"But what if they do?"

Tony looked blank. "We all scatter, I guess."

"You mean, we'd be in a chase with a police car after us?"

"That's about the size of it."

The car next to them was a rust-colored Pontiac with patches of gray undercoating on the door and hood. The driver turned to her and Tony and gave the thumb's-up sign.

Hope looked down at her hands and noticed that she was clutching her scarf so tightly that her knuckles were starting to feel achy. The other driver might think this was fun, but she certainly didn't.

So why was she there?

She glanced over at Tony. His eyes were glued on the starter, who was getting ready to unfurl a flag that looked suspiciously like someone's cotton undershirt.

"I hate this. I wish we hadn't come."

The words had come rushing out of their own

accord. But Hope knew she wasn't going to take them back.

Without a word, Tony put the car in first gear and rolled forward. "I've got a last-minute problem here," he told the starter. "We're dropping out."

They drove in silence almost all the way back to Tarenton.

"Are you angry with me?" Hope finally found the courage to ask.

"A little."

"I'm sorry you didn't get a chance to race."

Tony's smacked the steering wheel in frustration. "Who cares? I didn't even want to race. I just can't figure you out. First you bullied me into taking you up there. Then you change your mind at the last second."

"Bullied you? How can you say that?" Hope cried out.

She had never thought herself capable of bullying anyone — and certainly not Tony Pell.

"I didn't realize that you didn't want to go at all," she said. "I just thought you were afraid that I wouldn't fit in."

"Look who's talking. You say you'd like for me to meet your friends, but when I showed up at the game tonight it seemed as if you were in a big hurry to get me out of there."

Tony calmed down a bit. "Not that I blame you, considering what happened at the Pizza Palace."

Hope laughed. "It looks as if we've been talking in circles."

"You know what I'd really like to do tonight?" she added. "I'd like to go to that dance at the community center. How about it?"

Tony grimaced. "Actually, it sounds scary to me. All those kids think I'm a real hood. They're not exactly my biggest fans. But if you had the guts to come up to the race tonight, then the least I can do is keep my half of the bargain."

Walking into the dance was exactly like being the star of one of those E. F. Hutton commercials — the ones where everyone freezes the instant the sponsor's name is mentioned. The sight of Hope and Tony together seemed to have the same effect on people.

"We can leave if you want," Tony volunteered, noticing the way all eyes focused on them as they stood near the door, buying their admission tickets.

"No way," Hope told him. "I guess I must be getting used to this sort of thing."

And it was true. The old Hope would have been mortified to find herself the object of so much curiosity. By now, she felt almost used to it.

Fortunately, a set of slow dances started soon after they arrived. The lights dimmed slightly, and many couples who had been standing around, with nothing to do but look over the late arrivals, took to the dance floor.

"Well, here goes," said Tony, as he led Hope to a spot in an inconspicuous corner of the dance floor.

Surprisingly, since he drove with such confidence and athletic ability, Tony was an awkward dancer. Awkward, but not without possibilities, Hope decided. By the end of the set, he had relaxed a good deal and was actually starting to enjoy himself.

After that, things improved even more. During the first break in the music, Jessica and Patrick came over to say hello and chat for a few minutes.

The next to arrive was Holly Hudson. "I'm sorry I told Mrs. Oetjen that you shoved Diana," she told Hope. "The more I thought about it, the more I realized that your version of what happened was right."

Holly was a small, dark-haired girl, and she was wearing two dangling earrings in each ear and so much eyeliner that she reminded Hope of an over-eager raccoon. Even though she usually managed to be present whenever there was trouble, it was impossible to stay angry with her for long.

"I don't know why, but every time I start talking to Diana, I get involved in some kind of mess," Holly confessed. "I guess I'm just easily influenced."

"I know what you mean," Tony said ruefully.

Holly giggled. "I guess we have something in common."

Holly ended up offering to give Tony an impromptu dance lesson, and soon they were laughing so hard that some other seniors came over to join them.

"That wasn't so bad," Tony told Hope when they left the dance about an hour later. "You're friends aren't as stuck-up as I thought they were. Even Jessica Bennett seemed nice, and I always thought of her as the ice-princess type, I guess. Of course, I've met her boyfriend before. He used to have a cycle. Now he's doing pretty well in the moving business, I hear."

"H & T's TLC Moving! *That's it!*" Hope gasped.

"That's right," said Tony, perplexed. "So what's the big deal?"

Hurriedly, Hope repeated the conversation she'd overheard while she was waiting for the race to start.

"I was so upset about being at the race that it didn't really sink in," she explained. "All I knew for sure was that those guys were scary, and it wouldn't be good for me if they knew I overheard. But don't you see, it must be Patrick's van they're planning to hijack!"

Tony looked uneasy. "Are you sure? Maybe you misunderstood."

"Of course I'm sure. We've got to tell someone. We've got to go to the police!"

"Hey. No police." Tony shook his head vehemently.

"But why not? Those men are going to steal the antiques that belong to the auction barn. If we don't stop them, someone could get hurt."

"Maybe not. Maybe they were talking about something else altogether. You were so jumpy you probably let your imagination get carried away."

"It was not my imagination!" Hope protested. "What's wrong with you?"

"I'll tell you what's wrong." They had reached the Chang house, and Tony pulled the car over to the side of the road, in a spot just beyond the reach of the streetlight that illuminated the Changs' driveway. "Exactly how are you going to explain to the police what you were doing out there in the park? We weren't supposed to be up there at all. And if we hadn't been there, you wouldn't know any of this. So it isn't our responsibility, see?"

"No, I don't see! That's crazy logic, Tony. I don't want to get into trouble any more than you do. But we have to take the chance. Otherwise, whatever happens will be our fault. What if someone gets hurt?"

"Someone will definitely get hurt if we go to the police. And I'm not just talking about you and me. What about the other people who were up there? Don't you think the police will want their names? I may not be a candidate for the good citizen of the year award, but at least I know enough not to snitch on my friends!"

Hope was ready to argue some more, but just then she saw the lights in her mother's studio blink on and off several times. Then the light inside the garage came on and stayed on. She checked her watch nervously.

"Good grief," she gasped. "It's after one o'clock. My mom doesn't get angry often. But when she does, she's a lot scarier than the police, believe me."

"In that case, you'd better get inside quick," Tony told her. "I've had enough new experiences for one evening. I think I'd just as soon put off facing your mother till another time."

As Hope opened the passenger door to jump out, Tony reached over and gave her a quick hug. "I hope I didn't get you in trouble with your folks," he said. "Tell your mother I'm sorry we were so late."

To Hope's relief, her mother was not as upset as she feared. She accepted Hope's story that she had been at the dance ever since the game and had just lost track of the time. "You've always been so trustworthy and responsible," Caroline Chang said with an affectionate smile. "I guess anyone can forget to call once."

Trustworthy! The word almost made Hope flinch. What would her mother think if she told the truth? And what if she had ended up involved with the police?

Wearily, Hope took off her clothes and changed into her oldest robe, a heavy quilted wrap-around that always made her feel snug and comfortable. She had so much to think about, she was sure that she had a long night of soul-searching ahead of her.

But she was wrong.

Thinking that she would just rest a few minutes to clear her head, Hope stretched out on top of the covers and closed her eyes. A wave of exhaustion washed over her.

When she woke up, it was eight-thirty Sunday morning.

CHAPTER

Olivia Evans opened her eyes late on Sunday morning, knowing that she had run out of excuses. Coach Engborg was still in Haver Lake Medical Center, but the word was that she might be released any day. If she didn't get over there soon to visit her, she would miss her chance. The coach's feelings would be hurt, and she would never be able to think of an excuse good enough to set matters right.

Determined not to chicken out of the visit again, Olivia quickly showered and blow-dried her short hair until it looked its softest and fluffiest. She pulled her favorite sweater from her bureau drawer — the rose-colored one that always made her feel confident and cheerful — and finished off her outfit with a proper-looking pleated skirt of gray wool.

Before going into the kitchen to fix herself a cup of mint tea, she paused to study herself in the larger mirror behind the living room couch. Duffy was always teasing her about not looking her age. At least today he would have no excuse for saying that she looked twelve years old. She certainly didn't look like a kid today. She looked grown-up — more grown-up than she felt at the moment.

As soon as her tea was ready, she dialed Duffy's number. "Remember your promise to come with me if I wanted to go visit Coach Engborg?" she asked him. "How about going today?"

"This is one promise I don't mind keeping," Duffy told her when he picked her up at her house forty minutes later. "I'm glad you finally realized that there's absolutely no reason for you to avoid this visit."

Olivia laughed. "I wouldn't go that far. I still feel that I let the coach down. If anything, I feel guiltier than ever since I haven't been able to get along with Mary Ellen."

On the way up to the coach's room, they stopped into the hospital gift shop. Olivia considered buying a small bouquet of roses, but Duffy suggested a paperback murder mystery instead. "Knowing Coach Engborg," he said, "that will cheer her up more than any bunch of flowers."

When they got upstairs, Olivia was thankful for Duffy's advice. The coach's room looked like a combination florist shop and office. Ardith Engborg was sitting up in bed, looking alert and very busy. Her knee was supported by a wicked-looking sling arrangement designed to keep it as still as possible. But the rest of the bed had been converted into the coach's temporary desk. There were stacks of books and papers piled on top of the covers and on the nightstands. The rest of the room was filled with flowers, so many that the nurses had started setting them directly on the floor.

"I'm glad someone finally had the sense to bring me a good thriller," the coach said grate-fully when Olivia presented her gift. "Staring at flowers isn't entertaining for very long. I'm going crazy with boredom here."

Olivia couldn't help smiling. In spite of her bad knee, the coach was certainly her usual tough self. She spent a few minutes talking to Duffy about his latest articles for the sports section of the *Tarenton Lighter*. Then she dismissed him with a wave of the hand so that she could talk to Olivia alone.

"All week long, I've been feeling that I let you down," the coach said.

The words were so similar to the opening line that Olivia had been silently rehearsing that she almost wanted to pinch herself. "I don't get it," she said.

"I should have realized that Mary Ellen step-ping in for me would create tensions," Coach Engborg explained. "But I suppose I was so eager to do something to help her that I didn't give enough thought to how it would affect you."

Help Mary Ellen? Olivia had never thought of Mary Ellen as the sort of person who needed help. Ever. Tall, blonde, and confident, Mary Ellen was a natural star. Compared to her, Olivia had always felt like something of an impostor — a bit player who had blundered into a lead role as the captain of the cheerleaders.

And now that she was married to Pres Tilford, the only son of Tarenton's wealthiest family, surely Mary Ellen was set for life.

"I know what you're thinking," Coach Engborg said. "But believe it or not, marriage is not the solution to all of life's problems.

"Has it ever occurred to you," the coach went on, "that leaving New York and coming back to live in Tarenton took a lot of courage? Even though Mary Ellen had made up her mind that the decision was right for her, there were bound to be people who thought of her as a failure. Mary Ellen has the ability to be a good coach, and a good teacher. But right now she needs a boost to her confidence."

"I never thought of it that way before," Olivia admitted. "I guess I was too worried about myself."

Coach Engborg dismissed the apology with a wave of her arms. "Mistakes are never wasted if you're prepared to learn from them," she said, repeating one of her favorite sayings. "As for now, I'm counting on you and the rest of the squad to make this afternoon's demonstration at the sports clinic a success. I know you'll do your best."

127

Olivia promised that she would. She only hoped that her best would be good enough, because even though the coach had been doing her best to keep informed, there were more problems with the squad then she knew about. Mary Ellen and Jessica were feuding. Peter and Tara were disappointed that their suggestions for routines hadn't been accepted. Sean had been unusually quiet all week long.

But by far the worst problem at the moment was Hope. Olivia knew that Hope would never have walked off the floor during the game to talk to Tony unless she had something very serious on her mind. Was Hope in some sort of trouble? Unthinkable as that would have been a week earlier, it now seemed like a good possibility.

Back at the Dubrow house, Sean was beginning to wonder whether the sports clinic demonstration would ever come off at all.

His father had promised to help him pick up the cheerleaders' gear and take it over to the elementary school for the sports clinic. But now, at the last minute, he was backing out.

"I meant to help you out," Mark Dubrow apologized, "but I've got to finish these reports for tomorrow's sales conference."

"But Dad," Sean protested, "you were the one who insisted on helping me in the first place, remember? I was going to ask Peter, but you said you were coming to the demonstration anyway and you might as well give me a hand."

"You don't have to rub it in," Mr. Dubrow

said in a hurt tone of voice. "You know I don't like to let you down. But business comes first. You know that."

Sean wanted to remind his dad that he'd had two weeks to work on those sales reports. But that would have been pointless. By now he was used to his father's unofficial motto: Never do today what you can put off till tomorrow.

He loved his father. Still, there were more and more times lately when he felt that he was the grown-up of the family. And who needed that?

With only one pair of hands to do the job, and Sean's Fiero for transport instead of his dad's roomier car, transporting the cheerleaders stuff took much longer than he'd counted on. When he got to the school, Peter Rayman and Kate were on the front steps, looking anxious.

"It's about time, Dubrow," Peter groused. "You were the one who wanted me to be here at noon to set up the mats. So where were you?"

"Calm down. It's no big deal," Sean grumbled, half blinded by his armful of pompons. "My dad let me down again, that's all."

"Tell me about it," Peter snapped.

Kate flashed Sean a dirty look, and he realized that the remark was not a very tactful one to make to Peter. Peter's father had left home years ago and was living in California with his second wife and his new family. He was in touch with Peter from time to time, but he had never shown any great interest in spending time with his oldest son.

Sean thought of apologizing, but he decided

that there was no way to say anything without making matters worse. So he and Peter worked together in uneasy silence, unrolling the heavy mats and pulling them into place.

By twelve-thirty, the others had begun to arrive.

Mary Ellen and Jessica were both prompt as usual. But they stood at opposite sides of the gym, barely acknowledging each other's existence.

Tara surprised everyone by being all but paralyzed with stage fright. "I know I'm usually the biggest ham on the squad," she said, "but little kids scare me. What if they don't like me? I guess I'm always worried that little kids will see through to the inner me."

"So what's wrong with that?" Kate asked innocently.

Tara rolled her eyes. "The mere fact that you can ask that question shows that you're more sincere than I am. Your inner self and your outer self may match up. But mine don't. At least, not always."

"That's right," Sean joked. "Tara is just pretending to be a gorgeous, sexy redhead with a dynamite personality. Really, she's dumpy and frumpy, with all the charm of a wet dishrag."

Kate laughed, but Tara let out a groan, as if Sean had discovered her guilty secret. "One more crack like that," she threatened, "and I'm going to hide out in the women's room all afternoon."

"Don't you dare!"

The order came from Olivia, who had arrived just in time to size up the situation and see that a pep talk was in order. Calling the cheerleaders together, she gave a wholehearted pep talk. "The coach is counting on us to make a good showing today," she reminded them. "So let's put our personal problems aside and give this everything we've got."

Olivia's lecture worked magic. When the cheerleaders' turn came to do their demonstration, they put on a dazzling display of herkies and straddle jumps, cartwheels and walkovers. Then Peter had the inspired idea of getting up a group of parent volunteers and teaching them a simple routine. The parents had a good time, and the grade schoolers thought it was hilarious to see their moms and dads waving pompons and kicking in unison.

Then it was the kids' turn to try some stunts. Everyone worked hard. But it was Tara who was really outstanding. When the kids were divided up by age, Tara had volunteered to take the youngest group, figuring that they would be the least likely to notice how scared she was.

Soon, however, she realized that the kids were too uncoordinated to do the sort of moves the others were trying. "I'll tell you what," she improvised, "let's all pretend that we're animals. For example, I may look like a girl, but secretly, I'm really a chicken."

Tara demonstrated by strutting around the mat, clucking loudly and pumping her elbows. "Now let's see what kind of animals you are." Almost immediately, the members of the group were taking turns doing their imitations while the others guessed which animal they were seeing.

"You were the hit of the demonstration," Olivia told Tara when it was all over.

"All of you did a fine job," Mary Ellen added. "And I'm sure I was as nervous as all of you put together, including Tara. I never realized how hard it was to stay on the sidelines. I feel exhausted."

"Well, you've earned the rest of the day off," Kate told them. "You were the hit of the demonstration. Everything went perfectly."

"Except for one thing," Mary Ellen said to the group after Kate left. "I'm worried about Hope. She never showed up."

"You did say that this wasn't mandatory," Olivia reminded her. "Maybe she just changed her mind about coming today. Maybe she had homework."

"I'm afraid not." Mary Ellen shook her head. "I called Hope's house just before the demonstration started. I thought maybe she needed transportation. I spoke to Mrs. Chang, and she sounded really worried. She said that Hope came in late last night and then left the house early this morning without leaving a note to say where she was going. For some kids that might not be so unusual. But you know Hope. It just isn't like her."

"If you ask me, this has something to do with Tony Pell," Tara predicted. "I've known there would be trouble ever since Hope started hanging around with him."

"Let's not jump to conclusions," Jessica warned. "They could have gone for a ride. Or to see a movie. There are all kinds of perfectly normal things they could be doing."

Peter had been doing his best to stay out of the conversation. If Hope preferred the company of someone like Tony Pell, that was her business. He saw no point in making himself miserable by worrying about it. But what Jessica was saying made no sense to him. "No way," he said, contradicting her. "Hope wouldn't miss a cheerleading event just to see a movie. Even Tony Pell couldn't get her to do that."

"I don't see how it could hurt to drive around, take a look and see if we can find her," said Sean. "Kate and I will come back for the equipment later."

"Good idea," agreed Jessica. "I'll come with you."

While Sean, Kate, and Jessica piled into the Fiero, Tara offered to take Mary Ellen, Olivia, and Peter in her car.

"I'm sure this is unnecessary," Mary Ellen fretted as they pulled onto the highway. "We'll find Hope having a hamburger somewhere, and then she'll be angry with me for making a fuss."

Tara was about to reassure Mary Ellen when she heard the sound of a siren coming up fast behind her.

"Good grief!" she exclaimed, pulling the Chevy over to let the police car go by. "What kind of an emergency could there possibly be on a Sunday afternoon in Tarenton?"

"I don't know," said Mary Ellen, "but that car just turned down High Street. That's where Patrick's is. Let's follow it and see where it's going."

"Now I really do think you're turning into a worry wart," said Tara. But she dutifully signaled for a right-hand turn. Behind her, he saw Sean make a right turn, too, and she realized that Jessica must have had the same fear.

CHAPTER

The police car sped down High Street, made a sharp swing sideways, and came to a screeching halt, blocking off the street to further traffic.

Straining to see what was going on, Tara spotted another blue and white state police car a block down the street, and two more cars that may have been unmarked police vehicles. Then, just beyond them, she saw the H & T moving van.

Back in Sean's car, Jessica recognized the van at almost the same moment. "Patrick is supposed to be driving that van today," she cried out. "Where is he? Does anyone see him?"

Both cars pulled to a stop. Everyone piled out and started rushing toward the van.

"Stay back! Stay back!" the state police officer ordered them. "This is a crime scene here. We've got enough to do without a bunch of rubber-neckers hanging around."

"I'm Mary Ellen Tilford," Mary Ellen said,

mustering her most dignified voice. "I'm a good friend of the owner of that van. And my husband is working with him today."

"Sorry, but you'll still have to stay back until I check out what's going on," the policeman said. "I just got the call myself."

Their disagreements forgotten, Mary Ellen and Jessica stopped side by side. Sean, Olivia, and Kate hovered nearby for moral support. Peter and Tara, meanwhile, had moved onto the sidewalk and climbed onto a low stone wall to get a better view of what was going on down the street.

"Uh-oh," gasped Tara. "Do you see what I see?"

"I sure do," Peter agreed.

Standing near the first police car on the scene were two young men, one very tall and the other one much shorter. Both of them were dressed in jeans and camouflage-patterned down vests — and handcuffs.

Tara and Peter, however, were staring at the unmarked police car just beyond. Sitting in the backseat were Hope and Tony!

"What do you suppose they're doing here?" Tara gasped.

"No idea," said Peter. "But I bet this fuss has something to do with the antiques Patrick was supposed to be delivering today."

Tara and Peter stared at each other, their mouths open in shock. Both of them had remembered that Hope was in the group when Jessica told them about the delivery.

"Isn't that too much!" Tara said. "Hope Chang hijacking a van! Isn't that too much!"

"Be serious," Peter said, looking disgusted. "I'd never believe that of Hope. But come to think of it, I'm not so sure about Tony. I just hope he hasn't gotten her into trouble with the police."

Almost before she had finished speaking, the police started to lead away the two guys in handcuffs. One of them looked back over the shoulder at the unmarked car and waved his fist. "We won't forget you, Tony!" he yelled. "This is all your fault."

Just then, Peter saw Patrick emerge from the back of the van. "Everything's okay," he told one of the state police officers.

Jessica saw him, too, and went running past the police line and into his arms. Mary Ellen, following her, saw the familiar pattern of Pres's favorite red and black plaid jacket and old tweed cap, and grabbed him from behind, giving him a big hug.

"Uh, excuse me."

Mary Ellen jumped back. The jacket and hat were Pres's all right, but the person wearing them was a total stranger.

"See," Patrick told the stranger, "I told you that you looked enough like Pres to fool anyone, and I was right."

Seconds later, the real Pres Tilford came out of the garage. "What are you guys doing here?" he asked. "Hope said you'd be busy with the clinic open house until at least three o'clock."

"What are *we* doing here?" Jessica and Mary Ellen repeated in unison.

"You're the one who's got some explaining to

do," said Mary Ellen. "And what does Hope have to do with this?"

"It was all her idea," Pres said, grinning mischievously. "You'll find out the whole story. But not until I get a pizza. I'm starved."

The squad did find out everything, but not until the truck full of antiques had been delivered to the auction barn and the police were finished with their reports. By four-thirty, everyone was together again at the Pizza Palace, sitting around two large pies — one with anchovies and one without.

"When I woke up this morning," Hope was explaining, "I knew I had no choice. I had to tell the police about what I'd heard. It took all the courage I had to walk into that police station. Then when I'd told them everything, they started acting as if they didn't believe me. Then I got really worried."

"I don't get it," Tara said. "Why didn't they believe you?"

"Because Tony was already there," Hope explained. "He'd told the police the whole story, but he pretended that he was the one who overheard those guys planning the hijacking. So when I came in, the police started thinking the whole thing was some sort of prank. 'Okay, little lady, you've had your fun, now you go on home,' the police officer said to me."

Tony helped himself to his third slice of pizza. "You should have heard Hope let the poor guy have it for calling her 'little lady,' " he chuckled. "She seemed to grow about eight inches taller right in front of my eyes. She was so indignant, they actually started to take her seriously."

"But why did you ever take the van out if you knew those guys were waiting to hold you up?" Jessica wondered.

"That was my idea," Patrick admitted. "I talked the police into letting me help set a trap. And since Pres had already volunteered to help out his old partner, he decided he should stick around for the excitement."

"Excitement! I think you're crazy," Jessica put in. "It's a good thing I didn't know about it."

Pres shook his head. "Nothing to it. Patrick had a good idea and it paid off. And if he hadn't helped catch these guys today, they'd just try to rob him again some other time."

"Pres is being too modest," Patrick said. "He helped think of the plan. And then Hope came up with the idea of having that young state trooper, Rogers, dress up as Pres."

"What did you do then?" Tara asked. "Did you have to fight them?"

"Hardly." Patrick laughed. "Actually, they made it really easy. We saw them parked outside the garage, trying to look inconspicuous. So we just moved the van out onto the street, then pretended that we'd forgotten something back inside the garage. Those guys saw the van left alone and they thought it was their lucky day."

"But they were wrong," said Tony.

"Thanks to you," Patrick said. "I heard that fellow threaten you. I hope you don't get into any trouble for our sakes."

Tony shrugged. "I'm not worried about him. I know that guy, and he's all talk.

"What does bother me is that I'm going to be out of a job," he added. "I had to explain to the police what I was doing at the lake, and that means that there won't be any more racing there for a long time. Some of those racing nuts were good customers of the garage, and they won't be very happy with me."

"That's outrageous," said Sean. "They can't fire you for telling the police the truth!"

"Want to bet? Besides, my boss won't put it that way. He'll just say I had no business being up there in the first place. Which is true."

There was silence all around the table. Finally, Patrick got up and stretched. "I think I'll get another round of sodas. Want to help me, Pres?"

"You need help carrying a few sodas?" Pres asked incredulously.

Everyone laughed. Patrick had never been a weakling, and since he started his moving business he had become more muscular than ever. He was full of energy, too. At the moment, he looked as if he could pick up the entire freezer that the sodas were stored in and carry it across the room on his back.

Pres, on the other hand, was lounging in his seat, looking so laid back that just getting up would take a major effort. No one was a better worker when there was serious work to be done. But as soon as the crisis passed, he was the picture of relaxation.

"Come on, Pres. Get up," Patrick urged him. "I want your advice."

Patrick led the way over to the freezer, and he and Pres held a whispered conference.

"What's the big mystery?" Tara wondered aloud.

A few seconds later, they were back. "I was wondering if you'd like to come to work for me," Patrick asked Tony. "I could use some steady part-time help. Of course, it wouldn't be skilled mechanic's work. But I do need someone trustworthy like you."

Tony looked suspicious at first. "This is a joke, right?" he asked. "Trustworthy is not a word I hear very often. Not applied to me, anyway."

"It's no joke," Pres assured him. "You saved Patrick — and everyone — a lot of headaches today. Not to mention that someone could have been hurt. I can't think of anyone *I'd* feel more confident about having around."

Tony beamed. "In that case, Patrick, it's a deal. I only have one condition."

Patrick frowned. "What's that?"

"Can I bring Muttsy around?" Tony asked. "He's gotten awfully used to being around people."

"Sure. Why not?" said Patrick. "I could use a mascot."

Mary Ellen laughed teasingly. "And Muttsy is a perfect name! He'll fit right in at H & T's TLC Moving."

When the group broke up, Tony drove Hope home in the Mustang.

"I can't believe how my life has changed in just a few days," he told her. "First I met you. Now I have Muttsy, and a job working for Patrick

141

Henley, a guy who hardly ever spoke to me before. Suddenly, I'm even trustworthy!

"But meeting you was the most important part," he added. "I never thought a girl as sweet and as special as you could ever like me."

In the late afternoon light, Tony's eyes looked bluer than ever. Hope couldn't help feeling that those eyes had the power to bore right through the surface of things and see people's innermost feelings.

But did she want Tony to know her innermost feelings?

She still wasn't really sure. Did she like Tony for himself? Or had she just gone out with him because she was in the mood to be a little bit wild and rebellious?

"I'm really sorry that I got you into such a spot and made you lose your job," she said.

"No problem. It all worked out okay. We were lucky that the police were so interested in hearing about the hijacking that they lost interest in us. And now that they caught those guys redhanded, they don't need us anymore. Besides, it was my fault for telling you about the races in the first place. I was just trying to impress you."

"You didn't have to do that," she said automatically.

"Really?"

Uh-oh, thought Hope. From the way Tony was glowing over that remark she could see he'd taken it the wrong way. He thought she meant that he didn't need to impress her because she liked him so much already.

For the millionth time, Hope wished that she didn't find it so hard to communicate with boys. When she liked one a lot, she was so nervous about being rejected that she acted like a stuck-up princess type. But when she felt she didn't have anything in common with a boy, she tried so hard not to show it that she ended up giving out the wrong messages.

While Hope desperately tried to think of what to say next, Tony thought her silence meant that she was in a romantic mood. Impulsively, he took her in his arms and kissed her.

Tony was a great kisser, Hope had to admit. But was there that magic spark that would have made the kiss special? She didn't know.

And he noticed it, too.

"Sorry," he said, withdrawing to his side of the front seat. "I guess I misunderstood."

"I'm the one who's sorry," Hope blurted out. "In spite of the mess we almost got into, I had more fun this week than I've had for a long time. The trouble is, I just don't know whether or not I feel that way about you. I need time to think it over."

"If you have to think it over," he said, disgusted, "then it's a lost cause. There are some things you don't need to study. It's not a homework assignment. You just know."

"Maybe that's true for you," Hope protested. "But it isn't for me. And I have to do things my way. I can't help how I feel. I hope you're not angry. . . ."

"Of course, I'm angry," he snapped. "You

seemed to like me. Then, now that I've decided I'm crazy about you, you tell me that you really don't know how you feel."

"Oh." The sound came out of Hope's mouth like the air escaping from a punctured balloon. She knew Tony was right in a way, at least that was how he must see it. She just wasn't used to being criticized so bluntly.

Tony said nothing for a while, then reached over and patted her hand comfortingly. "Forget what I said, okay? I'm not angry with you so much. I'm just disappointed. I wouldn't want you not to tell me the truth. Your being so honest is one of the things I really like about you. A lot of girls would just pretend. Or else they'd make up some excuse to make me think it was my fault and they'd changed their mind about me."

Honest!

Not that there was anything wrong with being honest, but Hope wished just once that someone would tell her he liked her because she was sexy . . . or exciting . . . or glamorous. She was pretty sure that guys didn't tell Tara Armstrong they liked her because she was so honest!

Since there seemed to be nothing more to say, Hope unlocked the car door and started to get out. Tony stopped her by tightening his grip on her hand.

"I'm not giving up on you," he said. "You're the one who taught me that it's wrong to give up, right? So I'll be around. Maybe I'll even help you make up your mind."

Hope opened her mouth to say something, but

Tony touched a finger to her lips. "Don't answer me now," he said. "Just wait and see."

He drove off, and Hope stood on the street in front of her house, hugging her down jacket to keep warm. Tony could say things that were so infuriating! And for someone who had the reputation of being a loser, he could be awfully arrogant, too.

"You make me so mad!" she said, shaking her fist in the direction of Tony's departing car.

So why did she have that silly smile on her face?

There were some things she'd never figure out, not even if she thought about them for a hundred years.

Back at the Pizza Palace, Jessica and Patrick were in the small H & T van that Patrick still used for transportation, warming up the engine.

"I'm glad to see that you and Mary Ellen made up," Patrick remarked as he fiddled with the choke.

"That's right," said Jessica. "I stopped feeling resentful of her when I realized it was you that I was really mad at."

"When will I ever learn? When will I ever learn to keep my big mouth shut?"

Jessica couldn't help giggling.

"Okay. Do you want to tell me what I did wrong?" Patrick asked.

"It's not so much one thing you did," Jessica explained. "It's just that lately I've been feeling like the caboose on the Pres Mary Ellen-Patrick express. I know they're your friends, but I'm dating you, not Pres and Mary Ellen. All they ever want to do is hang around their apartment watching videotapes. That's fine for them, but I get bored. Besides, I'd rather spend more time alone with you."

"I'll second that," said Patrick. He flashed that slightly crooked smile that Jessica found so irresistible. "Actually, I've been thinking the same way. I guess I just figured everyone else was happy, so I'd go along. And I especially agree with that last part."

"What last part?"

"About wanting to be alone more."

Now they were getting somewhere. Jessica's mind was suddenly filled with visions of the good times they could have together. Just the two of them. Going dancing . . . seeing some movies that she liked, for a change . . . or even just staying home together, but at her house, where they could have some privacy to snuggle on the couch without Pres interrupting them at crucial moments to serve soda and popcorn.

She was about to put some of those visions into words, when she looked at Patrick and saw that he was making what he liked to call his "Dracula face." His lips were pulled back in an insane grin. His eyes were crossed in a way that made him look all too convincingly like a lunatic. "I vant to be alone vit you," he leered. "Because I am ze tickling maniac."

Jessica tried to keep a straight face, but she was so ticklish that the mere mention of the word was enough to set her into fits of laughter.

"You are really impossible, Patrick Henley," she said, when she finally managed to compose herself. "Sometimes I can't figure out why I'm in love with you."

The words were out of her mouth before she could call them back. Of course, she did love Patrick. She loved him more than she'd ever loved anyone. But was she *in* love? She considered those words too important to use lightly, and so far she'd managed to avoid using them.

Now she had actually said them. But Patrick seemed oblivious to the importance of the moment. "No doubt it's my magnetic charm and good looks." He surveyed the interior of the van, taking in the frayed upholstery of the seats and the scarred dashboard. "Also my taste in vehicles."

"Right," said Jessica.

Her serious mood had vanished, but there was still a long Sunday evening ahead of them. And plenty of time for them to be together, just the two of them.

Sean, Kate, and Olivia were standing next to his Fiero when they heard Jessica and Patrick, giggling like little kids inside the cab of his van.

"Listen to those two," said Sean. "I never figured Jessica would go for a guy like Patrick. I thought she would be attracted more to the suave type. You know, someone who drives a sports car and wears the right clothes."

"Someone like you, you mean," Kate pointed out.

"Right," said Sean.

Although he tried to act modest, he did think of himself as just about perfect, at least as far as appeal to the opposite sex was concerned. At least he knew now when Kate was teasing him, even if he wasn't always entirely sure he understood why.

"I was wrong about Tony, though," he said when they were inside the car. "He's really not a bad guy. And I guess we all should have trusted Hope more."

"At least everything turned out all right," said Kate.

"Right," Olivia agreed.

Olivia was genuinely happy for Hope, of course. Still she had to admit to herself that Hope's problems had helped to take her mind off her own. As long as Hope was the weak link in the squad, she hadn't worried too much about Mary Ellen's hint that Coach Engborg was planning to hold tryouts for alternates.

Now, almost at once, her doubts came flooding back. Did the coach really have faith in her? Or were the tryouts part of a plan to undermine her position as captain?

And if there were tryouts, who would be chosen?

What if it were that troublemaker Diana? Or Holly?

Olivia had never thought of herself as an ambitious person. Sure, she'd wanted to be squad captain. But that had been mostly a matter of pride because she was the only holdover from last year's squad. Then, right from the day she was chosen, she'd had doubts about her ability to do the job.

Lately, though, she'd started to realize just how determined she was to hold onto her leadership. Just the thought of a challenge to her job made her brown eyes burn with fierce determination.

No one, she promised herself, was going to push Olivia Evans out of her rightful place as captain of the squad.

Suddenly, Olivia felt that she could hardly wait to see Duffy.

She had no sooner formed the thought in her mind, than she caught sight of the old Ford that Duffy sometimes drove when he was on assignment for the *Lighter*. The Ford turned into the parking lot, and Duffy jumped out and ran up to Olivia, giving her a big hug.

"Are you okay?" he asked. "I just heard there was some trouble at the H & T, and that you guys were around."

"I'm fine," Olivia told him.

She could see that Duffy had been really worried. That was amazing in itself: Super-cool David Duffy always found a way to turn every crisis into a source of entertainment. Nothing bothered him. Or at least, he never showed that he was bothered.

"I can't believe you're so upset," she said aloud.

"Of course I'm upset." Duffy hugged her again. "I was worried about you. Besides, if you have problems I want to be around to face them with you. Don't you know that by now?"

That was good to hear. Olivia snuggled against

Duffy's tweed topcoat. Duffy's clothes always smelled of the brand of men's cologne he wore — that comforting blend of pine forest and a scent that was vaguely leathery.

It would be so easy, Olivia thought, to forget all about her resolutions and just lean on Duffy for advice and support. For a minute, she was tempted. But just for a minute.

"Remember what we were talking about just before the coach had her accident?" she asked him. "When you were asking me about my greatest fear?"

"I remember," he said. "But why talk about that now?

"Because I just realized something. I always thought my worst fear was that people will realize I'm not a leader. You know, that they'll see I'm just scared, shy Olivia — an impostor who's just pretending to belong with the popular crowd."

"But you do belong!" Duffy protested.

Olivia nodded. "That's just it. Maybe sweet, shy Olivia isn't the real me after all. Maybe there's another me. One that really enjoys being the center of attention. An Olivia Evans who won't let anything stand in the way of success."

Duffy grinned. "That doesn't bother me. I'm sure I'd like that Olivia Evans just as much."

"I hope so," she sighed. Because she had the feeling that the other Olivia Evans, the fighter, was going to be around more often from now on.

At least Duffy wasn't worried. The familiar mischievous gleam was back in his eyes. "As long as you're ready to continue our interview," he joked, "let's get back to the other questions you wouldn't answer that day. For example, the one about your favorite fantasy. I can't wait to hear all about it."

She laughed. "You really have a one-track mind."

"Where you're concerned, I do," he said.

Olivia gave him an impulsive kiss on the cheek, then slid into the passenger seat of the silver compact car. Everyone's troubles seemed to have worked themselves out. Hope was part of the group again. She and Jessica and Mary Ellen were all friends. And besides all that, she had Duffy.

But how long was all that togetherness going to last? She just wished that she could feel as sure as Duffy did that none of their feelings were ever going to change. But being the captain of the squad had taught her one thing — not to borrow trouble. For now, she was happy. And she was going to enjoy it.

What happens when a new cheerleader joins the squad? Read Cheerleaders #35, MOVING UP.

Pass the word!

Order these NEW titles chosen with you in mind!

- ☐ 33556-1 **THE BET** by Ann Reit $2.25 U.S./$2.95 CAN.
- ☐ 40326-5 **BLIND DATE** by R.L. Stine $2.25 U.S./$2.95 CAN.
- ☐ 40116-5 **DISCONTINUED** by Julian F. Thompson $2.75 U.S./$3.50 CAN.
- ☐ 40251-X **DON'T CARE HIGH** by Gordon Korman $2.50 U.S./$3.50 CAN.
- ☐ 33551-0 **HAPPILY EVER AFTER** by Hila Colman $2.25 U.S./$2.95 CAN.
- ☐ 33579-0 **HIGH SCHOOL REUNION** by Carol Stanley $2.25 U.S./$2.95 CAN.
- ☐ 40292-7 **THE KARATE KID: PART II** by B.B. Hiller $2.50 U.S./$2.95 CAN.
- ☐ 40156-4 **SATURDAY NIGHT** by Caroline B. Cooney $2.50 U.S./$3.50 CAN.
- ☐ 33926-5 **SEVEN DAYS TO A BRAND-NEW ME** by Ellen Conford $2.25 U.S./$2.95 CAN.
- ☐ 32924-3 **THIS STRANGE NEW FEELING** by Julius Lester $2.25 U.S./$2.95 CAN.
- ☐ 32923-5 **TO BE A SLAVE** by Julius Lester $2.25 U.S./$2.95 CAN.
- ☐ 33637-1 **WEEKEND** by Christopher Pike $2.25 U.S./$2.95 CAN.

Scholastic Inc.
P.O. Box 7502, 2932 East McCarty Street, Jefferson City, MO 65102

Please send me the books I have checked above. I am enclosing $_____ (please add $1.00 to cover shipping and handling). Send check or money order—no cash or C.O.D.'s please.

Name_____

Address_____

City_____ State/Zip_____
Please allow four to six weeks for delivery. Offer good in U.S.A. only. Sorry, mail order not available to residents of Canada.

PO1861